PRAISE FOR

You Are Free

"In *You Are Free*, Danzy Senna trains her gimlet eye on the inter-section of race and family life, and the result is a richly nuanced, often funny, always provocative work of art."   —Jennifer Egan

"Danzy Senna's stories are beautiful examples of deceptive sim-plicity, which of course isn't simplicity at all. The tales are seduc-tive, lucid dispatches from contemporary life, but the undercurrents are electric and strange, and go on working changes on you after the book is closed."   —Jonathan Lethem

"Danzy Senna's probing and marvelous stories delve into the deepest layers of the human heart and psyche, all while showing us a multicolored, multiflavored, and, most important, multilayed world to which we all—lovers, mothers, nomads, strangers—could easily belong."   —Edwidge Danticat

"Searingly smart and profoundly satisfying. Senna's people are beautifully rendered . . . they are completely alive in the mind as one reads, they *inhabit* us: a woman finds herself longing for the sign of material success implied by her child's acceptance into an exclusive school, and we do, too; another worries about her boy-friend's apparent failure to notice or remark about the suicide of a colleague, and finds herself questioning her own life with him, and we are completely with her; still another has trouble accepting the divorce of a friend, and the friend's new woman, while her own relationship begins to erode. . . . These women and men are pal-pable and so well wrought that one loses the sense that one is reading a book . . . a very damn good book."   —Richard Bausch

"Dispatches from a glorious and terrifying dimension: motherhood. Senna has written about shifting identities before, but this time it's the divide between being childless and bearing children that makes her imagination crackle. . . . It's one hell of a book."

—Victor LaValle

PRAISE FOR

Caucasia

Winner of the Stephen Crane Award for First Fiction
Winner of the American Library Association's Alex Award
A *Los Angeles Times* Best Book of the Year

"Lucid and magnificent."

—James McBride, author of *The Color of Water*

"[An] absorbing debut novel . . . Senna superbly illustrates the emotional toll that politics and race take on one especially young girl's development as she makes her way through the parallel limbos between black and white and between girl and young woman . . . . Senna gives new meaning to the twin universal desires for a lost childhood and a new adult self by recounting Birdie's struggle to become someone when she can look and act like anyone."

—*The New York Times Book Review*

"Absorbing, affecting . . . Senna's dynamic storytelling illuminates personal revelations that are anything but black-and-white."

—*Entertainment Weekly*

PRAISE FOR

Symptomatic

"Extraordinarily original."   —*The Washington Post Book World*

"Senna's debut novel . . . was hailed as nothing less than a contemporary classic, with the author evoking comparisons to everyone from Ralph Ellison to Vladimir Nabokov. Her follow-up, *Symptomatic*, proves the raves were right on target."   —*Elle*

"Disturbing, sensual . . . a must-read."   –*The Seattle Times*

"Suspenseful, and the anguish her vividly realized mixed-race characters feel when confronted with hostility from both ends of the racial spectrum is, sadly, all too authentic."   —*Booklist*

"Thoughtful and exciting. Highly recommended."
   —*Library Journal*

You Are Free

·STORIES·

Danzy Senna

RIVERHEAD BOOKS

New York

RIVERHEAD BOOKS
Published by the Penguin Group
Penguin Group (USA) Inc.
375 Hudson Street, New York, New York 10014, USA
Penguin Group (Canada), 90 Eglinton Avenue East, Suite 700, Toronto, Ontario M4P 2Y3, Canada
(a division of Pearson Penguin Canada Inc.)
Penguin Books Ltd., 80 Strand, London WC2R 0RL, England
Penguin Group Ireland, 25 St. Stephen's Green, Dublin 2, Ireland (a division of Penguin Books Ltd.)
Penguin Group (Australia), 250 Camberwell Road, Camberwell, Victoria 3124, Australia
(a division of Pearson Australia Group Pty. Ltd.)
Penguin Books India Pvt. Ltd., 11 Community Centre, Panchsheel Park, New Delhi—110 017, India
Penguin Group (NZ), 67 Apollo Drive, Rosedale, Auckland 0632, New Zealand
(a division of Pearson New Zealand Ltd.)
Penguin Books (South Africa) (Pty.) Ltd., 24 Sturdee Avenue, Rosebank, Johannesburg 2196,
South Africa

Penguin Books Ltd., Registered Offices: 80 Strand, London WC2R 0RL, England

This is a work of fiction. Names, characters, places, and incidents either are the product of the author's imagination or are used fictitiously, and any resemblance to actual persons, living or dead, business establishments, events or locales is entirely coincidental. The publisher does not have any control over and does not assume any responsibility for author or third-party websites or their content.

Copyright © 2011 Danzy Senna
Cover design by Helen Yentus
Cover art by Lorna Simpson
Book design by Kristin del Rosario

First Riverhead trade paperback edition: May 2011

Library of Congress Cataloging-in-Publication Data

Senna, Danzy.
    You are free : stories / by Danzy Senna.
      p. cm.
    ISBN 978-1-59448-507-7
    I. Title.
    PS3569.E618Y68   2011
    813'.54—dc22
                        2010032721

PRINTED IN THE UNITED STATES OF AMERICA

10 9 8 7 6 5 4 3 2 1

For Henry and Miles

"Yes, I'm tired," she said. "And do you know a funny thing? . . . I've never understood anything in my whole life."

"All right," he said quietly. "All right, Aunt Emmy. Now. Would you like to come on in and meet the family?"

—Richard Yates, The Easter Parade

CONTENTS

You Are Free

· Admission ·

The letter was unexpected. Cassie stared at it for a long time as she sipped her coffee, trying to decipher a hidden clue, though the language was crisp, the message to the point. They had been invited for an interview.

You recently completed the first stage of the application process when you attended a tour of the Institute for Early Childhood Development. You have been selected for the second step—an interview. This is for parents only. Please arrange appropriate childcare. Your interview time and date are:

TUESDAY, FEB. 18, 2:00 p.m.

Please call to confirm your attendance.

Cassie headed across the wet grass to Duncan's studio, letter in hand. She peered in the window to see if he was working. He was sitting in front of his television eating a mango with a knife. She opened the door and stepped inside. He was watching a basketball game and lurched back in his seat. "Fucking foul! That was so over the line."

"Duncan."

He turned and looked at her. "I didn't hear you come in."

"We got an interview."

He stared blankly.

"At the Institute."

He squinted. "The Institute?"

They'd toured the place two weeks ago and already he'd forgotten.

"The fancy school."

"Oh yeah, that." He turned back to the game. "Speaking of children, where is ours?"

"Brittany took him to the park."

"Well, then, you should be working. This is our window. Time's a-wastin'."

"I know," she said. "But this letter. What should we do about the interview? They've offered us a time and a date."

"How kind of them."

"Duncan. I'm serious."

He turned around slowly, his mouth glistening from the mango. "We aren't interested, remember? So an interview would

be a waste of time. Cody is already all set to go to Wee Things."
He swiveled back to the television.

Cassie bit her lip and stared at the back of Duncan's head.
It looked egg-shaped and vulnerable from the back.

It was true that they'd only gone on the tour because she'd
said she needed to research the play she was writing. She still
had no more than the barest sketches of the characters and
situation: a wealthy Los Angeles family, a disconsolate bulimic
wife, an eight-year-old girl's suicide attempt. She had not yet
decided whether the attempt would be successful.

She'd half believed the research excuse herself. But as
she'd driven them over to the Institute that morning in the old
Subaru—Duncan grumpy that he'd had to put on clothes—she
had to admit that she was weirdly, secretly excited.

Several of the mothers in her playgroup had briefed her
on the application process, which was famously mysterious and
daunting.

"You have to be a Spielberg or something to even get an
interview."

"I heard Will and Jada got wait-listed."

The Institute for Early Childhood Development. She and
Duncan had moved out west only recently from Providence,
Rhode Island; he'd gotten a teaching job, she'd gotten an NEA
grant for her next play. They were subletting a house—a friend
of a friend's—in Larchmont Village, a precious neighborhood
with a quaint, Mayberry feel to it, though it was on the edge of

West Hollywood and the residents were all film industry people. Cassie had already found a school for Cody in walking distance, but she'd applied to the Institute anyway, for research. She needed to know the rituals and mores of the city's elite. Anyway, the application wasn't hard, just a square white card with blanks for her and Duncan's names, their occupations, and their child's name, address, date of birth, and race. Hillary, a playgroup mother who had applied and been rejected twice, observed with some bitterness that the application was so bare-bones because the Institute got the rest of your information off the Internet.

"You have to be Google-worthy," she said.

The school was located in the middle of the city. It was across the street from a public school, an old brick building with brightly colored Spanish and English signs posted on the chain-link fence. The Institute looked more like a museum than a school—a sleek modernist building surrounded by a high cement wall lined with brightly colored turrets that stabbed the sky at odd angles.

"This better not take too long," Duncan grumbled as they approached the building. "I've got work to do."

She'd expected a small group of select applicants, but nearly every seat in the auditorium was filled, and the tension in the air was palpable. The crowd, on the surface at least, was diverse—black and brown and yellow and white, gay and straight. Duncan went for the muffins and coffee while she got on line for their name tags and a folder with information about the school.

They found seats in the middle of the room. Nearby she noticed a familiar face. For a moment she thought it was someone she knew, but no, it was a famous actress. She nudged Duncan. "Look who's sitting two rows down."

Duncan was leafing through the information packet. He snorted. "Check out the second question here." He was pointing to a green sheet labeled "Frequently Asked Questions."

QUESTION #1: "Is it true that all the children at the Institute are the children of celebrities?"

ANSWER: "No. Only a modest percentage of our parents are celebrities. We pride ourselves on our diverse community— which includes plenty of people you've never heard of."

The chatter in the room began to quiet as a small, zaftig white woman in an elegant blue pantsuit and clicking heels walked across the floor to the microphone and tapped it twice. Obedient silence fell over the crowd.

The woman smiled and spoke into the microphone. She had a vaguely European accent. "Welcome, parents. I'm Esther Vale, director of the Institute. I'm so pleased to see all of you here today."

She went on to give a speech about the school's pedagogy while the giant screen behind her showed images of the Institute children in action: an Asian girl frozen in hysterical laughter on the playground; a white boy with a mop of blond curls wearing safety goggles and staring at fluid in a beaker; a black girl onstage in a ladybug costume, her face alight with a gap-toothed smile.

The crowd around Cassie seemed to thrum, silently, with excitement and desire. She eyed their rapt faces as they listened to Esther Vale speak.

"Now I'm going to tell you who should not apply to the Institute," Esther was saying, a small, bemused smile on her face. "And I'm going to be honest with you. Can I be honest? You should not apply to the Institute if you don't see the value of our generous financial aid program that allows families of all income levels to attend. You should not apply to the Institute if you aren't interested in being an active member of our school community. You should not apply to the Institute if you are uncomfortable with nontraditional families—gay parents, single parents. You should not apply to the Institute if you are uncomfortable with your child making friends of different racial and ethnic backgrounds. You should not apply to the Institute if you don't want your child to have as much art—drama, painting, poetry, sculpture—in their curriculum as they have reading, writing, and arithmetic. If these aren't the qualities you want in a school, then this isn't the school for you, and there are plenty of private schools in Los Angeles that will suit your needs."

The crowd burst into applause as Esther strode off the stage. They had been given instructions to meet their tour guides at the front of the auditorium, based on the color of the sticker on their folder. Cassie and Duncan's sticker was blue and they joined the cluster around their group leader, a petite blond woman.

For the next forty-five minutes, she led them through the school — peering into classrooms, telling them about the amazing programs the school had to offer and her own children's experiences there. Duncan jiggled his keys in his pocket and kept checking his watch. Every so often they would pass another group of parents, and Cassie would recognize a face or a name on a name tag. She felt like she was in a dream. *There was Julia Roberts, and there was Donald Sutherland, and there was President Nixon . . .*

The last stop on the tour was the preschool area. Their guide explained that the window in the door was actually a two-way mirror, the kind used in police lineups. It allowed parents to come and watch their children as they worked and played. The parents in their group took turns stepping up to the window and peering through it at the class of toddlers.

"They're having snack time," the tour guide explained.

Cassie looked and saw a cluster of children sitting at a table eating what looked like edamame.

—— ·•◆•· ——

"I'm not impressed," Duncan said when they were safely outside the gates, heading toward their car. "The digs are fancy, sure, but there isn't anything special about the teaching. Sure ain't worth the insane tuition. Did you see the figures?"

"Esther said they have a generous financial aid program," Cassie said.

"Whatever. That's for poor people, their 'socioeconomic

tokens'—not for our upper-middle-class Negroid asses. Or did you forget, we made it, sweetheart. We on da East Side now." He pulled a muffin from his pocket, loosely wrapped in a napkin. He ate as he talked. "I'd rather send Cody to the school across the street. Did you get a peek at that? I wonder how Esther explains that little eyesore to all the Institute kids."

Cassie was silent as she pulled out of the parking space. She felt a burning of longing in her chest she couldn't admit to Duncan just now. She'd been impressed by the Institute—by the aggressively multicultural creed Esther professed, but also by the cheerful yet cloistered feeling of the hallways and classrooms. It seemed so civilized compared to the rough-and-tumble public schools she had attended growing up in Philadelphia. She wanted her child to grow up around *these* people, not *those* people, but she couldn't admit that to Duncan.

"So did you get all the details you need for your parody?" he asked.

She cleared her throat the way she always did when she was about to lie. "Yes," she said. "I think so."

<hr/>

And now here she was, holding this letter that invited them to go one step further. The Institute wanted to meet them. They were good enough to meet.

She didn't mention it again until later that night, after they'd had rugged sex. He was lying beside her in a postcoital coma when she said, "Duncan, baby, I'd like to do that interview at the Institute."

"I thought you finished your research."

"Not quite. I need the interview. It's the best part."

He sighed. "Okay. I guess we can go."

———— • ◆ • ————

Brittany was the only white nanny in the neighborhood. Duncan, who was originally from the South, had insisted on racial subversion—and he'd ended up with a "real live cracker," as he put it, an Alabama native who had been in Los Angeles ten years, fruitlessly pursuing a singing career while she cared for other people's children. Brittany was in her thirties and vaguely pretty, though Duncan said, "The dew is off the rose." He liked the irony of the situation: a black couple with a Southern white mammy caring for their brown child. Of course, they truly liked Brittany as well. More important, Cody adored her. He was even picking up her twangy accent.

"So, Brit," Cassie said, "we should be back from the interview in an hour. Can you give Cody lunch?"

Brittany sat still while Cody drove his Hot Wheels up her blue-jeaned leg, making a *vroom*ing sound.

"Sure thing, darlin'. Take your time. And break a leg!"

Brittany didn't know it was just research.

———— • ◆ • ————

The reception area was empty and Duncan sat playing a video game on his cell phone while they waited to be called inside.

"Can you put that away?"

"No, I'm winning."

She squirmed beside him, irritated. Moments later, a couple—a black couple, slightly ragged-looking, definitely "socio-economic tokens," as Duncan would say—came out wearing bashful smiles. They nodded at Cassie and Duncan but their smiles were tight and their eyes frightened.

A moment later, a middle-aged white woman came out to greet them, smiling with big teeth, her hand extended. "Hello, I'm Penny Washburn, director of admissions. Come on in."

She was rather sexless in the way of New England WASPs, with a long, thin face, graying blond hair, and bright blue eyes. She wore belted khakis, comfortable shoes, a pink oxford shirt tucked in.

They followed her down a plush-carpeted hallway to her office.

Inside, Cassie and Duncan took their seats. Cassie looked around. On Penny's desk sat a photo of two children—preteens with braces—who might be hers. Beside it was a framed picture of a smiling Barack Obama, which, silly as it was, made her feel more comfortable.

The interview lasted about twenty minutes. Cassie wasn't sure what she'd been expecting, but Penny's questions surprised her in their blunt specificity: When had Cody crawled? When had he walked? How long had he been breast-fed? How many words—approximately—did he have in his vocabulary? How did they choose to discipline him, if at all? What was his typical diet?

Cody was advanced in all areas, so Cassie felt a surge of pride as she answered. *Six months, ten months, thirteen months,* and *at least one hundred.* They disciplined him with time-outs and he ate a healthy diet, though a little heavier on cheese than Cassie would have liked.

"He's very precocious," Cassie said. "He already knows all his numbers and letters. Duncan thinks he might even be sight-reading."

"He's two, though," Duncan countered. "And an only child. Spoiled. Which means there are plenty of days when we'd like to send him back to the factory."

Cassie shot Duncan a dirty look. He didn't notice.

Penny, giving nothing away, nodded and scribbled in her notebook.

Then she wanted to know about their backgrounds, their work. Duncan told her about his paintings, the collage technique he used. Cassie was vague about her plays. Penny made interested sounds in her throat and nodded and scribbled more notes.

Then the interview was over and Penny was leading them to the door, wearing a placid, completely unreadable smile on her face.

Cassie breathed a sigh of relief when they were on the sidewalk. Though they'd only gone in the spirit of research, she had felt nervous, as if she were really trying to get her kid into the school.

"Penny seemed nice enough," she said when she'd started the engine.

"Whatever." ·

"It was cool she had a picture of Obama on her desk."

"Yeah, so what. He's the new Mickey Mouse." Duncan buckled his seat belt. "Anyway, are you finished?"

"Finished what?"

"With your fieldwork."

"I guess so," she said, and stared out the windshield at two women, one white and blond, the other Asian, mothers presumably, who were chatting on the sidewalk outside the school. The Asian one was familiar, from some television show maybe, though Cassie couldn't place her. They were both glamorous in high heels, with identical sheathlike hairstyles that fell across their faces. They made her think of Malibu Barbie and the ethnic Barbie, "Kira." She'd owned both in her youth. The women's matching silver SUVs were parked in the loading zone beside them. Two girls, their children, came striding out the gate of the school in matching Ugg boots, and waved goodbye to each other as their mothers led them to their respective vehicles.

———— • ◆ • ————

Cody was napping when they got home and Brittany was wearing her iPod and singing along to country music in a husky voice as she folded their laundry. Cassie told Duncan she was going out for a walk to think about her play. But once outside, she didn't think about it at all. Instead she went over and over every detail of the interview, trying to imagine what Penny had thought of them, how they'd come across. That slight and inscrutable smile—was it just what Penny's face did, or did it mean something?

She thought about the school—the vast splendor of it—and the schools she'd attended at that age, the children she'd known. Each child was tagged in her memory with a tragedy or a defect. Tasha in third grade—one of a handful of foster kids in the class—had worn a wig that all the kids teased her about. When Cassie's mother learned about the teasing, she scolded Cassie harshly, explaining that the girl's hair had been burned off by her very own mother. A tall white boy named Dougie had a big head and lived with his aunt and uncle in a trailer because his family had burned to death in a fire. Why had there been so many fire-related tragedies? Some of the kids she'd known had been mean and some had been nice, some had been funny and some had been cruel. Some had been quick as whips and others had been slow. They'd been good little fighters, all of them, when the situation called for it. The school had been diverse in a way—there had been white kids, black kids, Puerto Rican kids, a few Vietnamese kids—but they were all so dingy in her memory, a gang right out of *Oliver Twist*. Had they really been that dingy? And what had happened to them all?

She found herself on the street of the other school. Wee

Things Nursery. She headed up the block toward it. Apparently it was one of the oldest nursery schools in Los Angeles, and it was beloved. When they'd toured it months ago, Cassie had been charmed by it. She and Duncan had watched a group of toddlers sitting at their child-size table eating their bag lunches and drinking their juice, and Cassie had felt an unbearable tenderness and sadness at the thought of Cody joining them, joining the world beyond their home. They had been delighted when the director called to say there was a spot for Cody. It meant they could walk him to school every morning, and he would be only blocks away, in case he needed or wanted to come home early.

Now she stood in the shadows of a sycamore tree watching as parents picked up their children. They were not so different-looking from the parents at the other school—your basic upper-middle-class industry types. Their cars were mostly high-end luxury models. But now that she had a chance, a sliver of a possibility, of getting into the Institute, Wee Things had lost its luster. It looked run-down, slightly too hippie to be hygienic.

At home, Brittany had gone and Duncan was seated on the nursery floor with Cody on his lap. Cody stared up at him with huge black eyes as Duncan read from Dr. Seuss. It was Cody's favorite, *The Sneetches*. Cassie stood listening to the doggerel about the two factions, the Star-Belly Sneetches and the Plain-Belly Sneetches, the creatures identical to each other in every way except for this belly marking.

Neither father nor son saw her where she stood in the shadows.

———— • ◆ • ————

Then the preschool interview, along with her own work, faded into white noise in the back of her mind, because Brittany's mother went into a diabetic coma. Brittany had to go home to Alabama for a few weeks to tend to her, and Cassie learned what it was to be a full-time mother. From morning to night, she was manically caring for Cody—feeding him breakfast, brushing his tiny teeth, changing his diaper, wiping his butt, rushing him to the toilet to see if he'd poop there, and driving all over Los Angeles. Duncan helped when he could, but he was teaching two classes that semester. So Cassie hauled Cody from one mommy-and-me class to another, because sitting with a group of other mothers and children beat the tedium of sitting alone with him on the floor at home.

She found herself immersed in a world of mothers—women who'd had careers once, as actresses and scriptwriters, lawyers and businesswomen, women who'd gone to grad school, but were taking time off to be mothers. They were an unusual lot in that they could afford nannies but weren't relying on them full-time. Cassie, hanging on until Brittany came back, felt like a fraud in their midst.

Among the mothers, the question of schools almost always came up. It was an anxiety that every woman seemed to feel:

Where would her child land? Inevitably, the Institute came up too. Every one of the mothers wanted their child to go there. When Cassie pressed them as to why, they said vaguely, "It's just the best," or, "It's supposed to be amazing." They said it was a "feeder school" for the best grammar schools, which were feeder schools for the best high schools, which were feeder schools for the Ivy League. In other words, the Institute was a "feeder" for a life of success.

Mostly, though, they talked about how hard it was to get in, and every one of them had an anecdote they'd heard about somebody famous or powerful who had not gotten their child in, even when they'd offered the school some vast sum of money. The Institute, they said, never changed its mind. "If they don't want you, they don't want you." Then they would all sigh and move on to less depressing topics, like C-section scars or vaginal reconstruction.

One afternoon she slogged home through traffic with Cody after a tumbling class in Beverly Hills. He was tired and hungry and shrieking about some toy tractor he'd dropped in the parking lot, which Cassie had been unable to find. She was relieved to see Duncan's car in the driveway. She found him sprawled on the sofa watching television. She dropped Cody's hand, said, "He's all yours," and kept walking toward the kitchen.

She had the beginnings of a migraine. She gulped a long glass of water. She put it down and picked up the stack of mail on the counter. She flipped through some bills and then she saw it: a large white envelope from the Institute.

Her skin prickled. She picked up the envelope and tore it open. Her eyes flashed over the words:

Congratulations. Your son Cody has been accepted into our Toddler Program.

From the other room, she heard Duncan making monster noises, Cody squealing.

She went and stood in the doorway, watching them, the envelope in hand.

Duncan held Cody upside down. Cody was laughing hysterically. Duncan glanced over and caught her eye.

"You didn't tell me," she said.

"Tell you what?" he said, out of breath, letting Cody down onto the floor.

"We heard from the Institute." She didn't know what to do with her face, what expression to wear. She tried to smirk, but her mouth was not moving right. "We've been accepted."

"Oh yeah, I saw that. Well, la-di-da-da, ain't we special," Duncan said.

There were cartoons on the television; Cody went and stood directly in front of them, so that he became just a black silhouette against the manic flashing colors of the screen.

"I knew we'd get in," Duncan said, leaning down to pick the throw pillows off the floor and set them back on the couch. "That school is rich on money and poor on class. See, baby, we's culcha'd. We is some certified, authentified intellectuals, baby.

We stood out in a sea of celebrities and millionaires. You gotta love it."

She swallowed. "I wasn't sure we would. I mean, do you know the odds? Six hundred parents applied for twelve spots. At least admit to feeling a little, I don't know, surprised."

"I'm shocked, shocked," he said, deadpan, then brushed past her on his way to the kitchen. He picked up a bottle of wine and set to opening it. "It's gotta be five-thirty somewhere in the world." He said this same line every day at four-thirty. He poured himself a glass, leaned against the counter, and took a sip, watching her. "What's wrong with your face?"

"What do you mean?"

"Your mouth is all twisted funny. And your left eye is twitching."

She felt the pulsing now that he said it. She touched it gingerly. She tried to sound casual, nonchalant. "Listen, I know this isn't what we'd planned, but do you think we should consider accepting? I mean, it's supposed to be an amazing school." She realized as she spoke that she had been rehearsing this speech for the past two weeks. Somewhere in the back of her mind she'd been preparing these words. "I mean, once you're in, you're in through grade school. We wouldn't have to worry about schools again in two years the way we will at Wee Things."

He sighed. "Cass, we already have a school for Cody. A perfectly good preschool for a fraction of the cost. A sandbox is a sandbox. I refuse to pay out the ass for preschool. And did you read the fine print on the brochure we got on that tour? I did.

Each year the price goes up. And we have to buy insurance on our tuition because if something happens, if we decide to pull Cody out, they will not return our money. Yeah, because you have to pay the whole fucking year's tuition in one lump sum—because it's a school for people who have fifteen, twenty grand lying around in their checking account. Honey, they will sap us of every penny we have. No more trips to France in the summer. Shit, no more lattes with a side of biscotti. We will have to scale back—seriously—just so the kid can get to sit in a classroom with future Rich Fucks of America." He took another gulp of wine, a big one. He'd been preparing his speech too, she realized. Secretly, he'd been storing this up, preparing for this day, because secretly, they'd both known that they were going to get accepted.

"I know," she said. "I know all that. It's just—well, we got in. It's kind of a big deal."

"No it's not," he said. "We only went on the tour as a joke—remember? You were gonna write this acerbic parody about the stupidity and vapidity of American culture in the age of late capitalism. I line-edited your fucking NEA grant."

"But the thing is, I don't want Cody to rot away in a public school. I mean, we send him to public school and maybe he'll survive, maybe he won't. It's a wild card what will happen to him, what he'll become."

"It's a wild card everywhere, my dear. I'm sorry to inform you."

"No, not in the same way. This is where the world begins to divide. This is where the tone is set for the rest of his life."

"You sound like a *New Yorker* cartoon," he said with a chortle.

She felt the blood slamming against the inside of her head. She wanted to say, *Don't you dare take this from me, I'm almost there, I've almost made it to the other side, don't fuck this up for me.* But instead she said, "Not everything has to be a political statement, Duncan."

"This isn't about politics." He stepped to the window and looked out at the street, his back to her. "Have you ever noticed how boring and stupid kids from the fancy private schools are? Have you ever met one of those saps? They're like overbred puppies. They have no grit. Their limbs are all rubbery. Public school kids are scrappy, like pound mutts."

"Are you drunk?"

"No. Not yet." He sounded sober and calm. "I just don't want my kids going to the Institute—"

"What's the Institute?" It was Cody. He stood at the door, honey-colored, with a mop of shiny black curls.

"It's a school," Cassie said, squatting down to look at him eye to eye. "You're going to go to school soon, like a big boy, and your papa and I are trying to decide which one would be best for you." She paused, then said, "The big one or the little one."

"Which one has swings?" Cody asked.

"Both," Duncan said behind her. "They both have swings."

❖

The girl, Tasha, the one with the burned scalp and the crooked pageboy wig, ate her lunch alone every day. She was tall and big-boned and wore a strange assortment of clothes—sequined disco shirts during the day, sweatshirts with snowflakes on them in the spring, huge white no-name sneakers that the other kids called "bobos." They were clothes that Cassie learned at some point, she didn't know how, had come from charity. The other kids said Tasha smelled bad. Cassie got to test this theory once, when she was paired up with Tasha in English class. They were supposed to write a story together, using adjectives and adverbs, as part of a new program that paired advanced students with remedial students, rather than splitting them into separate classes. Cassie's friends laughed and pointed at her when they saw who she had been paired with. Up close, Tasha didn't smell bad, but when she bent over the desk to write a sentence, Cassie saw a patch of burned skin at the nape of her neck, pale and glossy and webbed, leading up to and underneath her wig.

———◆———

Duncan sat at the kitchen table across from her, watching as she made the call.

She jiggled her leg under the table. She felt nervous, angry, forced into it.

"Penny Washburn," answered a peppy voice.

"Hi, this is Cassie Rogers. My husband and I—"

"Cassie! Of course. I remember you and Duncan. Congratulations, you made it." She laughed. "I guess you know how difficult it is to get in. A lot of people would give their eyeteeth to be in your position."

"Yes, I know. We're so honored to have been accepted." Cassie looked at Duncan, winced, unsure all over again. This morning it had seemed clear, she'd woken and seen the light, remembered the play she was supposed to be writing—but now she was having second thoughts.

Duncan nodded his head and gestured for her to carry on as planned.

"So what's up?" Penny said.

"I'm really sorry, but we've decided Cody won't be able to accept your offer. It's, well, it's just that the schedule of the toddler program doesn't work for our, our lifestyle."

Duncan whispered, "Thank you and good-bye."

Penny was silent on the other end for a beat. "Oh. Well." She sounded surprised. "Are you sure?"

Cassie swallowed. No, she wasn't sure. But she felt Duncan's eyes boring into her and carried on. "Yes, we're sure. I'm so sorry. Perhaps we can reapply in a future year."

"Would financial aid help out? Would that change things for you? We have quite a generous financial aid program, as you know."

"I don't think so," Cassie said. "I don't think we'd be eligible."

"You'd be surprised," Penny said. "You'd be surprised at the range of income levels that are considered eligible here."

Cassie had not expected the conversation to go on so long. The school had a wait list a mile long. She had expected an icy thanks and good-bye.

"Thanks, Penny, but there are a number of factors influencing our decision. We're so sorry to have to pass on the offer this year. But I hope we can keep in touch."

There was silence. Cassie frowned at Duncan, who was sitting across from her, drumming his fingers. "Hang up," he whispered.

She raised a hand to shush him. "Hello? Penny?"

"Yes, I'm here." Penny's voice sounded strange—taut, as if she were holding in a cough. "So you're sure about this."

"Yes," Cassie said. "I'm sure."

"Okay," came a small voice. "Okay."

Cassie waited for Penny to say good-bye first, but when she said nothing, Cassie said, "Well, thanks, Penny. Bye."

Again, nothing. She hung up the phone.

"Jesus, that took ages," Duncan said. "What the hell were you discussing?"

"She was just making sure I meant it, I guess. I felt like she really was disappointed Cody wasn't coming."

"Oh, come on," Duncan said. "You saw the auditorium. Packed. She is calling her next set of parents right now and offering them his spot."

—◆—

At two in the morning she lay beside Duncan, listening to his breathing. The light coming through the window was gray, half lit by streetlamps. She could hear crickets humming. She had a pain in her stomach, a gnawing of regret.

Duncan Dickie was a black sheep; he was the only artist in a family of doctors. When she'd married him she'd been attracted to his strong opinions. She'd liked how he'd chafed at groups, anything smacking of mob mentality. He was what her mother called an iconoclast. But he had grown up in the bastion of the black middle class. As far as she could tell, the most traumatic thing that had happened to him as a child was being teased about his name. A bully named Eddie used to lead a playground chant. *When the weather's hot and sticky, that's no time for dunkin' Dickie. But when the frost is on the pumpkin, now that's the time for Dickie dunkin!*

He'd told her the story once, in the dark. He said she was the only person he'd ever told, as if the humiliation was still fresh.

Cassie had grown up poor, the daughter of a struggling single mother and a deadbeat father who showed up at some birthdays, drunk. Once in fifth grade, at recess, she'd been surrounded by a group of retarded boys, escapees from the special education class, who'd groped her. All her life she'd wanted to belong, to *have*, to possess what the other side possessed.

She sat up and stared down at Duncan's sleeping face. He was the problem. He was the barrier to her getting what she wanted—the perfect life. His face, even in sleep, had a kind of arrogance.

His eyes blinked open and he jerked, startled. "What are you doing?"

"Thinking."

He glanced at the clock radio. "About what?"

"About the school. The Institute. Did we just make a huge mistake?"

"Oh Jesus. Not this again. No, we made the right decision. Now can we drop it and get some sleep?"

"But it's the school everybody wants."

"Who the hell is 'everybody'? The ladies of Larchmont Village?"

"Nobody will believe it if I tell them we turned it down."

"So don't tell anybody."

She turned to her side and hugged her pillow, her cheeks warm with rage.

Duncan got out of bed. "Now I can't get back to sleep," he muttered. "I'm going to work in my studio." He left, sighing dramatically, and she lay there in the dark.

The problem with modern marriage was that everything had to be a consensus. Each choice had to be something they both wanted. For a moment, fear gripped her, a physical sensation—cold wetness under her arms, a dry mouth, a quickening of her heartbeat. *They had turned down the Institute.* She struggled to breathe. She felt as if she were falling into a long dark hole. She felt as if something large and warm and malevolent was pressing down on her, crushing her under its weight.

The next night while Cassie was sautéing garlic, the phone rang.

"Cassie," the voice on the other end of the line said when she answered. "It's me, Penny."

For a moment, she was confused.

"Penny Washburn," the woman clarified. "At the Institute."

"Oh, hi."

"Are you sure?"

"Excuse me?"

"Are you sure there's not something we can do to, well, make the offer more attractive?"

Cassie felt a momentary thrill. She turned off the heat under the saucepan. Duncan was out on the lawn reading a book to Cody. *The Sneetches* again. She remembered the arguments, the money. Duncan's position.

"It's so nice of you to call," she said, flushed, flattered. "Thanks for, well, for double-checking." She stared out at Duncan, her jaw clenched. "But yes, I'm afraid we've made up our minds. For this year anyway."

Penny went on. "It's just that I was about to offer your spot to somebody else, and I thought, let me just double-check. One more time. I'd hate for Cody to miss out on the opportunity, and I can't guarantee a spot next year."

Cassie felt a surge of doubt again. Was she sure? She saw Duncan rising and walking toward the house. "Yes, we're sure," she said. "But it's so nice of you to call. I realize how coveted these spots are."

This time the silence went on for so long that she thought Penny had hung up.

"Penny?"

"Yes, I'm just thinking. Listen. How about this: I'm not going to give your slot away tonight. It's too late. I'm going home. But let me give you my home number. If you change your mind, just give me a ring. I won't do a thing until tomorrow, say, after lunch."

She rattled off her home number before Cassie could find a pen. But she knew she'd committed it to memory.

Duncan came in the door just as she was hanging up.

"Who was that?"

She paused. "Nobody. I mean, just a prank call. Kids."

She told the lie automatically, without knowing exactly why.

"Kids still make those?"

"Apparently," she said, turning her face so he couldn't see her expression.

Duncan picked up a wine bottle and pulled the cork out. "It's gotta be five-thirty somewhere in the world, right?"

The next morning Cassie brought Cody to his music class. She went through the motions of singing along to the folksinger with him on her lap, then chatting with the other mothers afterward, but her mind was elsewhere. She looked up at the clock ticking on the wall and thought of her chance ticking away with it. When she got home it was already noon, and she felt a wave of sadness, as if something precious and irretrievable had been washed out to sea. She imagined Cody twenty years from now, in prison for grand auto theft, imagined herself leaving the jail after visiting hours. She thought about how she would look back to this decision as the cause of all his troubles. She imagined

Penny Washburn picking up the phone to call the lucky parents of the child who would go to the Institute instead. Her mouth tasting of metal, she imagined how they would celebrate.

The phone broke into her thoughts. She picked up, expecting Duncan.

"It's me, Penny."

"Oh. Hello."

"It's past noon," Penny said.

"I know."

"I was waiting for you to call."

"I thought I was only going to call if we changed our minds."

"And did you change it?"

Cassie felt a bug crawling on her arm and slapped at it, but nothing was there.

"I'm so sorry, but no." She felt strange, suddenly, unsettled by the woman's phone call. "We didn't change our minds. That's why I didn't call."

Penny sighed. "You know, a lot of families would give their eyeteeth to go here."

"Yes, I—I know that."

"So what's the hitch? The diversity issue? We're almost forty percent nonwhite."

"That's—that's great. That wasn't the problem."

"Then what was it?"

Cassie shifted uncomfortably, looked over the counter at Cody playing with his cars in the living room. She tried to remember Penny's eyes, her face, from their one meeting, but all she could remember was the picture of smiling Barack Obama on her desk. "I can't explain it."

She heard Duncan's car pulling into the driveway.

"Thank you," she said quickly, "for calling. I'm sorry it didn't work out."

She hung up without waiting for Penny to say good-bye.

She went onto the porch to greet Duncan, but once again— for some reason she couldn't articulate—she didn't tell him about Penny's call.

———◦◆◦———

The phone rang early the next morning, a shrill screech that cut through her morning haze as she set a bowl of cereal in front of Cody. Duncan was still asleep.

She looked at the caller ID. It was Penny's home number. She remembered it.

She didn't answer. She sat at the table, Cody slurping his cereal beside her, and watched the phone until it stopped ring- ing. She breathed out relief.

But a moment later it began ringing again. She went to it and stared down at it, as if it were alive.

———◦◆◦———

Later that morning, Duncan took Cody to swim class. It was a rare moment of aloneness. But just as Cassie sat down at her desk, the phone rang. She picked it up without checking the caller ID.

"The spot is still open," Penny's voice said. "We've been holding it for you."

Her voice sounded strange, muffled, and behind it Cassie could hear traffic, a car horn, distant mariachi music.

Cassie was frightened now, and didn't speak.

Penny said, "You're just the kind of family we've been looking for."

Cassie closed her eyes. She felt a pain like a mallet to her chest.

"Was it your husband?" Penny said. "Duncan Dickie?"

Cassie opened her eyes, breathed in sharply, and hung up the phone.

———◆———

The week went by without any more calls from Penny Washburn. She thought of telling Duncan about them, Penny's odd, desperate tone, but every time she opened her mouth, she stopped. It would seem strange to him that she hadn't said anything earlier, and she would have to explain that too, which she couldn't. She decided to put the whole episode behind her, just like Duncan was doing. It was a problem she had—she always regretted a decision after it was made, no matter what. She never could leave things be. She decided not to mention the Institute or Penny Washburn again as long as she lived.

She began work on her play. It was going slowly, but a character was emerging, the wife of a neurosurgeon. Nedra. Her name was Nedra. Pretty but woefully insecure Nedra. She was the type of woman who applied lipstick each night before getting into bed with her husband of fifteen years. Nedra was obsessed with her nose, convinced that it was the wrong shape and size. She would have several surgeries in the course of the play to "correct" it.

In bed, Cassie chattered to Duncan about her work. "She's going to be a sort of vehicle for me to discuss so much — race, sex, body dysmorphia. I see her as a kind of symbol of our times. Nedra. What do you think of that name?"

Duncan didn't answer. She looked up and saw he was fast asleep, his reading glasses still on his face.

———— • ◆ • ————

She read *The Sneetches* aloud to Cody one evening, snuggled beside him in his toddler bed. Outside was a rare heavy rain. The sound of it reminded her of her childhood, Philadelphia, real weather. She remembered her mother snuggled beside her on such nights, reading to her — the standard of happiness to which all other moments would be compared. Cody rested his head against her chest and brushed his fingers against her collarbone. She'd read the story to him so many times that she barely had to look at the page. The Star-Belly Sneetches were having a beach party, gorging themselves on hotdogs and marshmallows, while the sad Plain-Belly Sneetches stood watching, cold and bereft in the sandy gloom.

She realized that she too was comforted by the story, perhaps because it was so very familiar.

When she went to turn the page, she realized that Cody had fallen asleep. She could have slid him off her chest and turned out the light and left him there, but she was enjoying the feeling of his warm body pressed against her. Duncan was out back in his studio, working. Dinner was warming in the oven. She had only the salad to make. She closed her eyes. For some reason she thought about that girl, Tasha, the one with the burned scalp. Cassie's mother had made her promise to be nice to the girl. In fact, she had made Cassie promise to sit with her at lunch. But in the cafeteria the next day, seeing Tasha sitting all alone, Cassie had balked. She had hovered beside Tasha for a moment, holding her tray, but then had moved on to her table of friends. Later she told her mother about sitting with the burned girl. It was her first lie, or the first she'd been conscious of telling, anyway.

Distantly, she was aware of the sound of knocking. Somebody was knocking at the front door.

She slid Cody to the mattress and rose carefully, switching off the light.

Out in the front room, the knocking was hard and persistent. She went to the door and looked through the peephole.

A figure stood on the doorstep, tiny and warped, head turned toward the street.

Cassie opened the door.

Penny Washburn stood on the steps. The rain had flattened her hair, making her look gaunt and ravaged. There was a puddle around her sodden loafers and she was hugging herself, shivering. The air outside was cold and rain blew in on Cassie.

"Can I come in?" Penny's voice was plaintive, beseeching.

Cassie stared at her, unable, momentarily, to speak. She finally managed: "I'm sorry, but we were just about to sit down to dinner."

"Just for a few minutes," Penny said, hacking into her hand. "See, we've kept the spot open, there's still a place for you. I can give you a few more days to reconsider."

"We're not interested," Cassie said, sure of it now.

"Why not?" Penny emitted a sound—half sob, half laugh. "Just give me a reason. I don't understand. None of us understand."

From the back of the house, Cassie could hear the glass door sliding open, Duncan coming inside, whistling. She couldn't let him find her here, couldn't let him see how far it had gone.

"We don't want you," she whispered into the night. "The answer is no." She hesitated, then hissed into the lashing rain: *"Go away."*

She could hear Penny's bewildered shout, "Lots of people would give their eyeteeth—" before it was cut short by the sound of the closing door.

·The Land of Beulah·

The bitch was a mystery. She didn't look mixed, more like some breed that hadn't yet been discovered. Strangers on the street were forever trying to guess her background. They studied her appearance and behavior for clues, but with each guess her identity seemed to shift. In the face of such uncertainty, people saw what they wanted to see. Black folks thought she was mostly rottweiler. White people swore she was a Gordon setter. Puerto Ricans usually guessed an unlikely blend, such as German shepherd and miniature poodle, while the Arab guys at the bodega predicted she would grow into a wolf. The Korean grocer kept his distance, swearing she was the same kind of rare, vicious foxhound that had bitten him as a child.

Jackie wasn't sure who to believe, or whether she cared. Mixing, she understood, was a game of risk; a mutt could turn out pretty, or pretty damn ugly. The bitch had won at least that round of Russian roulette. She was lovely: shiny black fur, long satiny ears, and little brown dots above her eyes that gave her a perpetual look of fierce concentration.

———•◆•———

Jackie had stumbled upon the dog quite by accident, one autumn afternoon while she was out jogging. Brooklyn was almost beautiful that day, a frenzy of disparate colors along brownstone-lined streets. But Flatbush Avenue was as ugly as ever. Seasonless, it stretched out before her, a clutter of extinguished signs and dented vehicles. Jackie moved fast, trying not to notice the men who beckoned to her, gesturing to their loins as if offering fruit for sale. She kept her eyes fixed instead on a giant billboard ahead. It was an advertisement for Newport cigarettes, but there were no cigarettes in the picture. Instead, it showed an ecstatic black woman holding a pin to the gigantic pink bubble emerging from her boyfriend's mouth. His eyes were wide open in mock fright. The words across the bottom of the billboard read: "Alive with Pleasure!" Jackie found the image disturbing and looked away. That's when she glimpsed the puppy.

It stood out, incongruous, a spot of life amid the urban squalor. It was tied to a metal pole by an extension cord, so tightly that it couldn't properly sit or stand. Yet it grinned and squirmed excitedly at the sight of Jackie approaching.

Attached to the dog's collar was a piece of torn cardboard with a message crudely scrawled in orange marker: TAKE ME HOME, it said.

Jackie felt a surge of pity for the creature that took her by surprise. She reminded herself that the problem wasn't hers to solve. After all, there were stray mongrels all over Brooklyn, scrawny, mangy creatures who wandered through traffic, wearing brindled coats and crazed, terrified grins, searching for some pack that had long since disbanded. She'd heard on the news that the problem was worst in autumn. When the weather began to change, people grew tired of the puppies they had enjoyed all summer and set them loose on the city. Jackie had noticed them everywhere—in parks, under bridges, in doorways of abandoned buildings. She'd also noticed the women who saved them. Stray women. Jackie had glimpsed them around her neighborhood, wandering through traffic, wearing sensible shoes and foundationless faces, tugged along by a pack of dirty mongrels. Jackie wasn't one of them.

Yet as she stared down at the creature wearing the pitiful sign, she had to wonder if it had been placed in her path for a reason. She was recently single, unhappy, homesick for some land she couldn't quite remember. One year into her job search she was still temping. She lived alone. She exercised alone. She ate her dinner alone at night in front of rented movies. She occasionally went to parties alone and left alone, nobody with whom to talk over the evening. Sunday mornings were the worst. She awoke awash with grief, imagining a city full of couples frolicking playfully under puffy duvets, surrounded by newspapers and pastel mugs containing pale, sweet coffee.

Jackie leaned down and began to struggle with the extension

cord, attempting to free the puppy. She heard somebody yell, "Suckah!" and whipped her head around to see who had spoken. A grown man on a child-size bicycle cruised down the sidewalk in her direction. He leaned forward with his elbows raised to his sides like chicken wings, his knees pumping up to his shoulders. He didn't meet her gaze and she wondered if she was imagining things. But when she turned back to the puppy, she heard it again. "Suckah!" She looked over her shoulder, but the man had already whizzed past and was cruising down the hill, out of sight.

A few minutes later, Jackie stumbled up Fulton Avenue toward her building, carrying the trembling animal. She felt flushed with Good Samaritan pride and couldn't help grinning goofily at strangers. They didn't smile back. A teenage boy loitering in front of Kansas Fried Chicken shouted out, "Don't your dog know how to walk?" Farther up the road, two old Caribbean women shuffled past her and one of them muttered, "Now that's what I call devotion." Jackie sensed sarcasm in her tone, but she smiled anyway, as if the woman had meant it.

———— ◆ ————

It had been two and a half months since she'd been dumped. Kyle was his name, but everyone called him Kip. He was tall, light-skinned, and dreadlocked, with a mole the shape of Italy on the small of his back. He had gone to prep school all his life, and had only late in college discovered his negritude. Now he was a stockbroker. He claimed he wasn't really working for the Man: He was just making money so that later, when he joined the revolution, he'd have something to offer.

When Kip told her it was over, Jackie had been taken by surprise, but as she thought it over she saw that there had been warning signs. Every time he saw her he'd found fault with something about her: her feet were callused when he touched them, her breath smelled of garlic, she had a pimple on her chin. He had refused to hold her hand when they walked through black neighborhoods, explaining that while he knew she was black, strangers might think otherwise.

Jackie was the product of a black saxophone-playing father and a white soul-singer mother. She'd come out looking like the missing link between Sicily and Libya. Cabdrivers liked to claim her as part of their race just before they asked her if she was married. In the summertime, she was the color of well-steeped tea. In the winter, she was paler, as if a dollop of milk had been added, although her hair, a tangled mass of wiry curls, always gave her away. Kip had liked her to wear it out around her face, so that people would know.

Kip didn't believe in race mixing. He thought brothers who dated white girls should be called out in the street.

"But what if they really love each other?" Jackie had replied weakly, thinking of her own white mother and black father, who'd hated one another for as long as she could remember. "I mean, live and let live, right?"

He laughed at her and patted the top of her head gingerly. "There are casualties in every revolution."

He'd broken up with her at a soul-food restaurant in Brooklyn, over a shared dinner of ribs, greens, and macaroni and cheese. "You can walk away from this anytime," he said out of the blue, sweeping his arm around the restaurant, although she knew it was blackness he was referring to. "For me, there's no way out."

She rested her gaze on the baby-back ribs in front of her. They looked gruesome to her all of a sudden, evidence of a crime.

After Kip told her it was over, he walked her to the subway, chivalrous till the bitter end. It was cold outside, and an old man dressed in a three-piece suit stood on the corner nearby, waving a Bible and raving about homosexuality. Kip had buttoned up Jackie's coat in an oddly paternal gesture, then punched her lightly on the chin and said, "Don't worry, Jack, I'm doing you a favor."

She sucked her teeth and looked away. "What's that supposed to mean?" She longed for the comfort of her bed. She would cry later, under her duvet, out of his sight. For the moment, at least, she had to be hard.

Kip shrugged and stared at the ground, as if reading her future in the patchwork of chicken bones and candy wrappers. "Just wait and see," he said. "You'll end up with a white boy named Jake, an architect or maybe a painter. You'll move to Nyack together and live in a big farmhouse. You'll remember me as a phase you were going through. Just wait and see. Girls like you never stick."

Jackie wanted to remind him that it was he who was leaving her. But instead she simply listened and wondered if what he said was true. Would she end up with a white boy named Jake, in a farmhouse in Nyack? It didn't sound so bad, especially the part about the farmhouse, but she had tried to look disgusted by the life he'd described.

Hidden underneath the sign, hanging from the dog's collar, was a silver tag engraved with the name "Beulah." Strangely, the tag listed no contact number, as if the dog's former owners had wanted to ensure her identity, but not her safe return. Jackie vaguely remembered a television show her grandmother used to watch that starred a black maid named Beulah. The name seemed demeaning somehow, like Aunt Jemima. But it was the only name the puppy had. Jackie felt obliged to keep it.

She called all her girlfriends to tell them what she'd found. That was a mistake.

"I give it a week," said one.

"A dog in the city?" shrieked another. "Yuck, picking up shit ain't for me."

Another one warned, "Watch out. You know what happens when a woman gets a dog."

"What?" Jackie asked, with a stab of fear.

"She stops being lonely. And you know what happens when she stops being lonely?"

"What?"

"She stops looking for a man."

Jackie shook her head and told them all they were wrong.

But when she looked around her apartment, she felt a shiver of horror. A soiled maxipad had been shredded across the kitchen floor. Black paw prints were smeared along the white wall of the hallway. A shoe—a silver open-toed pump Jackie had worn at last year's birthday party—was now a mangled allusion to its former self. She tried to remain good-natured about it. She'd just saved a creature's life, after all. But she couldn't help feeling she was losing her grip on something she hadn't even known she was clutching until now.

That first evening, Jackie walked into her bedroom to find Beulah peeing on her bed, a yellow puddle spread across the snowy white duvet. The dog smiled up at Jackie with evident relief. Jackie felt something—a clicking in her brain—she'd never felt before. In one swift motion, she picked Beulah up by the scruff of her neck and flung her to the floor. The puppy fell with a thud, then rose, whimpering, to her feet. Jackie kicked her sharply in the ribs, so that she fell again with a yelp. Jackie hungered to do more, but Beulah ran out of the room, tail between her legs.

Later, when Jackie had cooled down, she found Beulah hiding under the kitchen table. She reached an arm out to pet her, but Beulah shrank out of her reach. Jackie spent the rest of the evening showering the puppy with affection—kisses, tickles, a bouncing ball—feeling that she'd never loved anyone more, and possibly never would.

She promised herself it wouldn't happen again. She had never thought of herself as ill-tempered, and she knew you weren't supposed to hit animals. She tried to be content with hissing obscenities at Beulah, but several times that weekend she lost control. She slapped the puppy on its butt when it tore her fancy sheets, and jerked its leash too hard when they went walking down the street, so that the puppy's body lunged from side to side. Jackie found that small acts of violence—harmless ones, really—helped to quell her rage.

Monday morning, Jackie dawdled around the house. She couldn't bear the thought of leaving Beulah alone. But if she didn't get to the temp agency by eight, all the good assignments would be taken. As she put on her panty hose, cheap pin-striped business suit, heels and lipstick, Beulah watched from a corner. Under the dog's scrutiny, Jackie's outfit suddenly seemed tartish to her, a whore's uniform. She left the dog food and water and toys, and whispered, "I'm sorry" as she went out the door.

At the temp office, black and Latino women of all hues were lined up in seats against the wall, filling out applications and sipping coffee from Styrofoam cups. Television sets blared from high in the corners, each displaying a different morning news personality. All the other temps were dressed to the hilt in four-inch heels and impeccable hairstyles. Jackie felt dowdy in her ill-fitting suit and scraggly hair. The temp agency had put out

43

several boxes of Dunkin' Donuts, but only jelly-filled doughnut holes remained. Jackie shoved one in her mouth and chewed unhappily as she waited for Vanessa, her agent, to find her work.

Fifteen minutes later, Vanessa—a whirling dervish of bottle-blond hair and orange polyester—came flying out of the office holding a clipboard. She scanned the row of female bodies, tapping her foot and snapping her gum in time. Jackie wondered, not for the first time, if she was coked up. Her eyes fixed on Jackie.

"Jackie!" she shrieked, as if they were old college buddies.

Jackie slumped low into her chair, embarrassed. She was always one of the first to get hired, no matter how late she arrived. She'd divined the pecking order immediately: lightest and whitest first. Dark-skinned girls were always the last to go, no matter how fast their typing speed. She kept her eyes to the floor as she followed Vanessa into the back office, not wanting to see the other women cut their eyes at her.

Vanessa sent her to a Swiss bank on Park Avenue, where she was tucked in a corner with a stack of loan applications to enter into the computer. Her trainer was a small beige man named Chuck. Most permanent employees treated temps with contempt, but Chuck was friendly—too friendly. He was giddy, like somebody who has been deprived of air and sunlight and has sat for too long in the same position. That morning he spent over an hour showing Jackie how to enter the loan figures into the computer, a task so simple it needed no explanation. He sat too close, his knee pressed against hers, and kept resting his clammy hand on her exposed elbow when he wanted to underscore a point. He smelled of printer ink. When he could find nothing more to tell her about the data, he shuffled back to his own cubicle, giggling—about what, she couldn't imagine.

If Vanessa had taught Jackie anything over the past year, it was to work at a turtle's pace. The longer you took with your tasks, the longer the job would last. You couldn't be too slow, or they would notice. Jackie had worked out a perfect pace—the pace of somebody competent but not particularly bright—but today she worked more slowly than usual, distracted by thoughts of the puppy. She wondered what Beulah was doing. She imagined her dressed up in Jackie's workout clothes, slumped human-style on the couch in front of a talk show, eating a bag of potato chips. She smiled to herself at the thought. She began to doodle a picture of Beulah in exactly that scene, but felt someone watching her.

She looked up. Chuck was smirking at her from his cubicle. His feet were propped on his desk, and he leaned back in his chair. He held a sweating can of Fresca at his waist, just above his crotch, and she glimpsed a distinct bulge beneath his khaki pants. When he spoke, his voice came out croaky, like an adolescent boy's.

"Did you get laid last night?"

She wasn't sure she'd heard him right.

"You have that post-fuck glow," he hissed.

The bulge in his pants seemed to move slightly. His own face glowed, like that of a wax figurine. She wondered what would happen if she held a match up to his skin, whether it would melt or burn.

He tilted his chair back at a more precarious angle. She watched him, willing him to fall and bite off his tongue. After a moment he seemed to see something on her face that made his smile disappear and the bulge in his pants withdraw from sight, like a gopher disappearing into a hole. He turned, quite abruptly, back to his computer, and Jackie could see that the tips of his ears were red. She too turned back to her screen, only to see her own reflection—pale, tense, her eyes dark hollows—staring out of its glassy surface. She whispered: "You've all been a terrible disappointment." She didn't know who the words were aimed at or what they meant.

On the way home from work that evening she stopped at a pet shop in the Fulton Mall. The mall was really just a street in downtown Brooklyn made up mostly of sneaker shops, sportswear stores, and fast-food restaurants. Jackie generally tried to avoid it. She called the mall Child Abuse Row, for its everpresent stream of teenaged mothers slapping their dazed children while Jackie looked on in horror. But Jackie remembered that there was a small, anemic pet shop at the far end of the mall, and she wanted to buy Beulah a gift to make up for leaving her alone all day.

The store was devoid of customers and smelled like a hamster cage, warm and dank and fertile. In the back sat a row of puppies—purebreds. They looked perfect, too cute, like the puppies of calendars and greeting cards. Jackie noticed how much calmer than Beulah they all were, almost languid as they stared at her from behind their plastic walls. She peered in at a beautiful golden retriever. It lay on its side, eyelids drooping. She tapped on the glass but it just blinked at her, unmoving.

Jackie wandered the chewies aisle, searching for gifts. There were piggy snozzles, along with pig's ears and hooves—a use for every part of an animal's body. She resisted the bully sticks—dried bull's penises—but left the store with a Nylabone, a piggy snozzle, and a little squeaking mouse doll in her purse.

She limped toward home, her toes crushed together in the tips of her work shoes, and wished she'd changed into sneakers at the office. All around her, women moved wearily toward their homes, and she felt herself to be part of a long and sad parade. It wasn't quite dark yet, the sky a swirl of light and dark purples. It looked heavy to Jackie, like a fruit swollen past edibility, on the verge of bursting. As she turned onto her block, it slipped into black. She breathed relief, released from some nameless dread.

———◆———

The living room was covered in white, like a cartoon vision of heaven. Beulah sat in the middle of the vision, grinning and slapping her tail happily against the floor. Jackie paused at the door, awestruck, imagining for a moment that she had died. Then she realized that Beulah had destroyed the down comforter, the one she'd already stained with pee.

Jackie dropped her purse filled with treats. Beulah wiggled

her way across the room to greet her, but when Jackie knelt down and held out her arms, the puppy shrank back, sensing something wrong. She was close enough that Jackie caught her by the scruff of the neck anyway. The puppy's tail wagged slightly between her legs—she didn't know if she was being greeted or punished, and Jackie wasn't sure either. Some small voice told her to control herself. She pulled Beulah close and stared into her face, trying to decide on the best punishment. It was then that she noticed the hole.

It sat directly between the dog's two nostrils—small but perfectly round, as if a thin nail had been driven through it, or a large needle. It looked almost as if somebody had tried to create a third nostril. Jackie felt first repulsion, then horror, then pity. How had she not noticed it before? She began to cry. She stood up, sniffling, backing away from the mutilated animal, who wagged its tail, panting.

"Who did this to you?" she hissed. "Who did it?"

She had the urge to call Kip, but she knew that was impossible.

The hole reminded her of shackles and chains, of mutilations too deep ever to heal. Jackie threw herself down on the bed and sobbed silently into her pillow. She felt a pain in her chest like a burn, and she was aware that it wasn't just the hole she was crying over. She whispered to herself, "It's going to be okay. It's going to be okay." After a moment she heard Beulah's toenails clicking down the hall. Beulah leaped onto the bed, where she wasn't supposed to be, and began to lick the salt off Jackie's cheek. Jackie held her close, gently this time.

— ◆ —

The bitch was crazy. She never slept. She never even got tired. At night, Jackie tossed and turned, listening to the incessant click of Beulah's toenails as she paced up and down the hallway. In Jackie's half-conscious state, she imagined the dog was supernatural, a laboratory escapee, and that the hole in her nose was where the scientists had inserted crack cocaine.

Later in the week, she asked the veterinarian, a tall WASP, whether the puppy was perhaps abnormal. The vet agreed with Jackie that the hole was mysterious—and disturbing—but she insisted that the puppy was just behaving like a puppy. She simply needed more exercise. She told Jackie about the dog gatherings in the center of the big park up the hill. Rain or shine, winter or summer, the dogs and their owners convened before nine o'clock, when leash laws went into effect, so that the dogs could tire themselves out running.

She took Beulah the next morning, before work at the Swiss bank. The dog owners stood in small clusters, chatting with one another under the cold white sunlight of late fall. Steam rose from their Styrofoam cups and disappeared into the crisp air. The dogs—there must have been at least twenty—swarmed on the grass around them, wrestling, fighting, humping, shitting, sniffing. Beulah pulled Jackie forward, trying to join the fray, wheezing from the pressure of the collar against her esophagus. Up close, the group looked like a cult. They wore expectant believers' faces, as if they were waiting for a UFO to land, or the Virgin Mary to descend from the clouds, and the manic dogs added an air of helter-skelter.

Jackie unhooked Beulah's leash and watched her romp over to a black Labrador with a red bandanna around its neck. They did their crotch-sniffing dance, then began to wrestle. Snippets of conversation—stray phrases from a whole new language— floated across the grass toward Jackie:

. . . you've gotta wait six months to spay . . .

. . . lost his Booda Velvet . . .

Can I have my Kong back, please?

Jackie heard a voice behind her.

"You must be new here."

She turned around.

The woman before her, swinging a leash in her hand like a lasso, was heavyset, with rosy cheeks and big horsey teeth. She could be a haggard thirtysomething or a young fortysomething. She reminded Jackie of a high school guidance counselor, somebody settled and sexless. She might have been pretty once; now she was practical and solid. She looked as if she had dressed in a hurry: filthy Harvard sweatpants, New Balance sneakers caked in mud or shit, a misbuttoned beige cardigan.

By the woman's side was the ugliest mutt Jackie had ever laid eyes on. Everything was off. It was barrel-chested, and its legs were meant for a much smaller dog. Its fur was no color at all. One of its eyes was completely opaque—a cataract?—and along its nose ran a raised scar. Its face wore a crazed joker's grin. It appeared to be more wild boar than dog.

The woman saw the look on Jackie's face. "I found him this way. About six months ago. Abused, bleeding, stabbed in the eye. Somebody did a real number on him. He had a tag that said 'Humpty Dumpty,' with a phone number, but I threw it out. Whoever did this to him didn't deserve him back."

"Oh." Jackie tried to think what else to say. "How good of you."

The woman stuck out a hand and said, "I'm Nan, by the way. Welcome."

Jackie introduced herself; then, for lack of anything better, she nodded in Beulah's direction, where she was being mounted, unsuccessfully, by a poodle. "I found my puppy a few days ago. She was a stray too."

Nan squinted at Beulah. "You *found* her? That's a good-looking stray. She couldn't have been on the streets for long." Jackie sensed a kind of one-upsmanship in the woman's tone.

"She has a hole in her nose," Jackie said.

Nan blinked at her. "So? I have two."

"No, an extra hole, somebody pierced her nose."

Nan shrugged, unimpressed, and then went on to offer unsolicited advice. She told Jackie where and when (eight months) to get Beulah spayed, and how to get the stray dog saver's discount on vet expenses. She told her what kind of food to feed her (Eukenuba) and how many times she needed to be walked each day (fewer than three long walks was inhumane). Jackie was hungry for advice, and she felt comforted by Nan's sensible enthusiasm. She seemed to know everything—about history, literature, dogs. She informed Jackie she'd been working on her PhD for ten years. She was writing her dissertation on Victorian methods of birth control. Jackie listened to Nan chatter while the dogs ran in circles around them. She felt happy for the first time in months.

The park was staggeringly beautiful in the morning light. The people continued to look expectant, as if they were waiting for something better to come, but the dogs were content, having already found perfection. The field was wide and lush, the sky unbroken by buildings. It was hard to imagine that beyond the green lay the filthy, groaning city. The park reminded Jackie of Narnia, the land that had so obsessed her as a young girl. She'd spent hours in her mother's closet, eyes closed, trying to walk through the closet's back wall and into another world. She'd been surrounded by the smells of her mother—nicotine and whiskey and jasmine oil—but for a second it had seemed that the wall really was melting away, giving access to another country.

Jackie learned a lot from Nan those first few weeks, the basic and not-so-basic facts of dog psychology.

Dogs travel in packs, unlike humans, who tend to couple.

Fifty percent of all so-called purebreds are actually mixed. The other fifty percent—the truly pure ones—are stupid and sickly, and susceptible to glandular problems.

Dogs have a denning instinct and therefore respond well to confined spaces. Paradoxically, they feel safe, rather than trapped, in cages.

Among dogs, hierarchy rules. There must be an alpha dog, somebody to follow; otherwise, the pack is lost.

In public, at the dog park, Jackie spoke with disdain about the unknown person who had tied Beulah up on the street. She nodded her head sadly when the other dog owners talked about euthanasia, puppy mills, dog abuse.

In private, Jackie continued to beat Beulah. Not every day, but nearly. It became a ritual, like a glass of red wine with dinner. Beulah barely seemed to feel it. She wore a bemused, mocking expression while Jackie went at it. She didn't seem in the least bit scared. But Jackie was—scared of herself, the way she hungered to hit the puppy. She would examine the house when she got home from work, searching for damage. She always found it, and then she would set upon Beulah with a newspaper or her hand, depending on the severity of the damage. It was like an itch, a tickle in her fist, the way she yearned for violence, and in the act of it felt exhilarated. Sometimes she was able to restrain herself, and then she would settle for cursing. *I hate you, you fucking dirty mongrel. You're ruining my life. Get lost. Get lost. Get lost.* But usually those curses were not enough. They didn't satisfy her.

The beatings didn't work either. Beulah continued on her path of destruction, undeterred by Jackie's raised hand. She ate Jackie's panty hose, broke the bathroom scale, peed on the wooden floors, and toilet-papered the living room. Jackie spent her small salary on bull's penises and pig's ears, but Beulah wanted more. She wanted to loot the bedroom closet, seize the objects most valuable to her master and destroy them.

Outside, Beulah was just as bad. Jackie had never noticed before that the streets of Brooklyn were paved with discarded chicken wings. They were everywhere, and Beulah loved them. She pulled so much on the leash that strangers often called out, "Who's walking who?" Off the leash, she never came when Jackie called her. Sometimes, Jackie was forced to chase her for the better part of an hour. Beulah would stand still, grinning, until Jackie was within inches, then at the last minute she would leap out of Jackie's reach and run in circles around her. It was as if she was trying to humiliate Jackie in front of her new friends.

None of this behavior was lost on Nan, who tried to give Jackie advice on training Beulah. *Spray her with water when she barks. Shake a can filled with coins when she jumps up on you. Spend fifteen minutes a day practicing commands. She must love and respect you as her alpha dog. All dogs long for a benign dictator.* Underlying all her suggestions was the smug refrain: *There are no bad dogs, just bad owners.*

Jackie pretended to listen to what Nan said. But really she

was thinking about how she was going to kick Beulah's black ass when they got home.

————◆————

Even as Jackie kicked and beat and cursed Beulah, she loved her. Beulah was all that mattered to her. Their relationship was one of extremes. Extreme hatred, extreme love. Jackie wondered if you could truly love something without sometimes despising it. Violence seemed just another form of intimacy.

She stopped going to Manhattan so much for dinner or movies. When she did, she spent the entire time imagining Beulah at home with her bone and the television blaring out a language she'd never understand. Jackie stopped jogging—Beulah enjoyed group exercise more, so Jackie took her place on the sidelines like a proud mama and watched her play with the other dogs. Jackie learned to almost enjoy evenings spent curled in a filthy heap with Beulah on the living-room futon, which was permanently pulled out now to serve as Beulah's bed.

Jackie began to lose touch with her old circle of friends—the pretty, manicured set of girls who lived in the city. She didn't miss them much. They had begun to annoy her, their constant prattle about men, dates gone wrong. There was something so desperate about their endless parties and fancy dinners, as if they were in a perpetual state of meaningless celebration. The last time she'd been out with them, still smarting from the breakup with Kip, she'd noticed how none of them looked at the others when they spoke. Instead, they looked over one another's shoulders, scanning the bar for eligible men. They were a sisterhood of fools, she'd thought, and she'd taken to avoiding them. If they assumed it was because she was depressed, in mourning—because her man had turned out to be a dawg, just like all the rest—they were wrong. The truth was, she was too preoccupied with Beulah to notice either his or their absence.

Jackie grew close to Nan. They spent most mornings and evenings together at the park, where they huddled close for warmth, watching their mongrels romp on the grass. It was an odd thing, the dog park. They were strangers, but there was an intimacy to their encounters, particularly in the mornings, before they had put on their business suits and makeup. They saw one another in their natural state, sleep still stuck to their eyes, the way lovers see each other before the day begins.

Nan, she learned, hadn't had sex in ten years. Her last "encounter," as she put it, was with her ancient thesis adviser. He'd been in his early seventies at the time but was now dead. "It's weird," Nan said, wearing an oddly elated smile, "you stop missing it after a while. You learn to live without it."

Nan liked to gossip nastily about the other dogs and their owners, although it was hard sometimes to tell which she blamed, the person or the dog. This one stole Humpty's Kong, that one didn't pick up her dog's poop, "making the rest of us look bad." She seemed to have had a bad experience with almost all of them at some point or another. She particularly hated a group of single, childless white women who, unlike

Nan, hadn't quite given up hope of partnering yet. Nan called them "the Weather Girls," after the early eighties disco duo famous for their hit single, "It's Raining Men." She said they were all waiting for the sky to rain hunks on them. "Fools," she'd spit out. "*Fools.*"

The Weather Girls all owned purebreds, and for this Nan hated them the most. Their dogs, being purchased, had the pretense of being status symbols, whereas Humpty and Beulah had the air of the tragic, the accidental, thus conferring on their owners a level of moral superiority. Nan liked to whisper mean things about the purebreds—how Dodo, the obese chocolate Lab, resembled a piece of walking shit, or how Edwina, the aged golden retriever, was essentially retarded, or Mindy, the cocker spaniel, was allergic to her own tear ducts. Nan particularly hated a Shar-Pei named Kabuki, who was owned by Doreen, the de facto leader of the Weather Girls. Jackie had to agree that Kabuki was funny-looking. His brown mass of wrinkles, like a crumpled fur coat, reminded Jackie disconcertingly of the disease that aged small children prematurely. But Kabuki didn't have a disease. He had been bred to look that way, a cruel hoax by a mad scientist.

Nan liked to point out that Kabuki would never survive if left to evolution. "He'll get a fungus infection between those folds in his fur that everyone thinks are so cute—and then he'll die of gangrene." Nan said Humpty and Beulah stood a much better chance of surviving in the wilderness. They resembled what she termed the "standard mongrel." Nan said that in the laws of Darwinian selection, the standard mongrel was the one that always survived: thirty to forty pounds, short floppy ears, long nose. Beulah's ears and fur were a bit on the long side for natural selection, but she'd at least stand a chance, unlike Kabuki.

Sometimes, when Nan wasn't around, Jackie would join the Weather Girls in conversation. They reminded Jackie of her friends in the city, the ones she'd stopped seeing. Those city friends were black, while the Weather Girls at the park were white, but they were basically the same model of woman. It struck Jackie that while she could be black or white, depending on how she decided to wear her hair, she was always a woman. There was no escaping that.

——— ·◆· ———

Winter came. The grass at the park turned gray and crunchy and the sky above appeared streaked and dirty, like the film that coated Jackie's apartment windows. For a while that autumn, even into December, the park had felt like a pleasant ritual for Jackie, but increasingly it felt like a drag. Often there was a tension in the air, and fights broke out regularly between the dogs and between the owners. The people seemed to forget, at times, that the dogs were animals. They would argue, viciously, their teeth bared, over whose dog had started the fight. Nan, meanwhile, had grown possessive. Several times, she'd invited Jackie to join her for a movie and dinner, and each time Jackie had declined, not wanting to expand their friendship beyond the realm of the park. If Nan caught Jackie talking to the Weather

Girls, she would sulk angrily on the edges of their circle and leave without saying good-bye.

Jackie dreaded these petty dramas, but she continued to go to the park. It was still the only way to tire Beulah out. And besides, Jackie no longer had any other friends. Her sisterhood of fools had stopped inviting her to dinner parties and barhoppings, and she'd stopped wanting to go.

Jackie began to eat only when she was hungry, and she gave no thought to taste or calories or nutrients. She would scavenge the dark streets around her house for takeout, settling for whatever was near and cheap—kung pao chicken and fried shrimp, pizza, beef patties, jerk chicken, or roti—and carry it back to her apartment, hunched against the cold. There, she didn't bother to put it on a plate, she'd just eat over the container it had come in, wolfing down what she could while Beulah stood waiting for leftovers.

Jackie no longer put much effort into her appearance. Her weekends went by without a shower or even a change of clothes. Her fingernails were filthy, her hands callused from the pull of the leash. Her feet, ordinarily scrubbed and toenails brightly polished, were as tough as hooves. The hair on her legs grew freely. She had never known how long and dark it could grow. She could see the women at the temp agency eyeing her with disapproval when she showed up for a new assignment. She was no longer Vanessa's favorite, no matter how pale her skin.

She'd hidden away her long mirror months ago, to keep it from Beulah. The pea brain was always jumping against it, trying to play with her own reflection, and Jackie had been afraid she would break it. One day, while rummaging through her closet for a tennis ball, Jackie came upon it. She pulled it out and propped it against the wall. She glimpsed herself full length. Just a few weeks earlier, she had taken to wearing her hair in twin braids, Pippi Longstocking style, so its texture was unclear. She wore her usual dog walker's uniform: Adidas sweatpants and a sweater with the logo of a trucker's union across the front. She had not gained or lost any weight, but she looked different: raceless and ageless, almost virginal. There was a rough clarity to her features she hadn't noticed before—a wide blankness to her gaze. Her skin was clear, her features bold. She put the mirror away, vaguely troubled, but not certain exactly why.

———— •◆• ————

One Sunday in late February, Jackie stumbled up Flatbush Avenue after Beulah on their way to the park, their weekend ritual. The sky was a flat slate gray, and the frigid wind burned her cheeks. She hadn't dressed for the weather, and her glove-less fingers were numb around Beulah's leash.

A couple in the distance caught her eye. They were unre-markable except that the man was black and the woman was white. The man wore jeans and a red windbreaker, his head shaved neatly to his skull. The woman was tall and blond and wore jeans and motorcycle boots. They spoke to one another conspiratorially, one head tilted toward the other. Jackie stared at them, thinking for a moment of her parents. She wondered if they'd ever been in cahoots that way.

When the couple was a few feet away, the man looked up. Only then did Jackie recognize Kip.

He looked good, better than when they'd been together. She'd always disliked his dreadlocks; they'd made him seem vain and girlish. She'd fantasized about cutting them off. His new short cut made him look more vulnerable, naked, as if all the illusions had been cut away along with the hair. He was laughing at something the white girl had said. Jackie could see the girl better now. She was attractive in a flawed sort of way, with a slightly hawkish nose and a large mouth. She reminded Jackie of all the white girls she'd ever grown to hate—the ones with a casual, moneyed confidence that always made Jackie feel awkward and prudish in their midst.

Beulah, straining at the leash, half dragged Jackie to a little plot of dirt where a tree was planted. She squatted and began to take an immense shit in her humpbacked position.

Kip was upon them now, and as he passed he glanced up casually in Jackie's direction. She held her breath, waiting for him to smile, or frown, or blush with embarrassment beneath the light brown of his skin. But he only looked past her at the dog, and sneered slightly. Jackie held a plastic bag tightly in her hand, and the sweat made it slippery. Kip's eyes moved over Jackie again, but showed no recognition.

They moved past her. She watched their backs as they strolled away down the avenue. A block farther on, she saw them disappear into a diner. She recalled going there once or twice with Kip, for a big bacon-and-egg breakfast after a leisurely morning in bed. Jackie leaned against the slender tree, but it bent back with her weight. Had Kip simply not recognized her, or had he just pretended not to notice her? She wasn't certain. She left Beulah's mess where it was, just this once, and followed Beulah up the street.

The dog park was more crowded than usual; the atmosphere was raucous. Balloons and a small folding table had been set up in the center of the grass, and music played from a portable tape deck. The dogs and their owners crowded around the table, talking and laughing. Kabuki wore a pointy party hat. Jackie remembered Doreen mentioning something about Kabuki's birthday party. Nan had whispered afterward that she wouldn't be caught dead at such a ridiculous event. They'd laughed about it together. Now Jackie could see that some of the dogs were trying to get the party hats off by pawing at their heads, but most of them were gathered in front of the folding table, where the owners were doling out treats, just like at a real toddler birthday party.

Beulah romped off to join the group. Jackie watched as one of the Weather Girls waved to her, then attempted to get a party hat on Beulah's head. Another one of them spotted Jackie and shouted, "Join the fun!"

Jackie pretended she hadn't heard and shoved her hands in

her pockets, looked at the ground. She couldn't help thinking about Kip and the girl. She imagined them getting married someday, beginning to look alike over the years, the way couples often did. She imagined they'd have children who looked like her—butterscotch babies. She could rouse no anger. The idea of their union was oddly comforting.

She must have stood thinking a long time, because when she looked up, the park was empty. The party had disappeared. The only evidence that anybody had been there was a lone party hat on the grass, and a bright orange balloon stuck high in a distant tree. The cold had turned Jackie's face into something foreign and rubbery. She could no longer feel it. She looked at her watch. It was way past nine. Leash laws had gone into effect. She would get a ticket if she didn't comply.

In the distance she spotted Beulah. The dog darted ecstatically through the trees, hatless now, a lone speck of black and brown, oblivious to the cold and to her master.

Jackie called softly. "Beulah, Beulah, Beulah."

Then a bit louder—*Beulah!*—the way they beckoned the maid on the TV show her grandmother liked to watch.

Beulah heard that one. She turned, her ears pricked up. She grinned, wiggling her bottom in excitement, then pranced behind a cluster of trees. She wanted to play tag. She wanted to humiliate Jackie once again.

Jackie felt a dull clicking in her brain, a throbbing in her gums, and swore she'd kick the dog's ass when she caught her.

She'd beat her right here, in the dog park. She didn't care who saw her. Nan could call the cops for all she cared. There *were* such things as bad dogs, not just bad owners. It went both ways.

She began to stride across the grass toward Beulah, her hands clenched into fists by her side, but halfway there something went out of her. She felt tired. Her throat hurt and her chest ached, as if she were coming down with something. She watched Beulah in the distance as she ran insane circles around a tree, faster than seemed possible. She ran so fast she blurred, so fast it almost looked like there was more than one of her, like the tigers in *Little Black Sambo*, who ran so fast they turned into the butter that Sambo, along with his mother and father, Mumbo and Jumbo, slathered onto pancakes for their triumphal meal. Jackie imagined herself chasing Beulah until both she and the dog turned into butter. She too would melt and disappear.

She spoke the dog's name one more time in the weakest of whispers. *Beulah.* Then she turned and trudged away, up the slope of mud and grass toward the big road. At the cross-walk, she felt something heavy shift inside of her, a sense of dread stronger than she'd ever felt before, and turned to look behind her—but the dog was not there and the feeling was gone as quickly as it had come over her.

———◦◆◦———

She lay on a table in the back room of a midtown salon. She was on her lunch break from her new temp job at a law firm. A Russian woman stood hunched over her, concentrating on her eyebrows. She was giving Jackie an expression of perpetual surprise. Odd, Jackie thought, that women sought to look shocked. Not coy or delighted, but shocked. It was as if they wanted to look frozen in the moment just before something happens.

The Russian woman was artificially pale, all bleached out. Her dye job seemed to mock her dark, Asiatic complexion. She didn't talk much, but when she pulled up Jackie's skirt to start waxing her legs, she whistled through her teeth.

"When the last time you wax?"

Jackie glanced down at her body. Her legs looked strong and useful, unintentionally toned and muscular. It had been months and months since she'd touched them.

The woman shook her head, then took the spatula and stuck it into the pot of warm wax. She stirred it for a minute, then spread the wax along Jackie's leg, like butter on bread. It felt nice, warm and soft, but quickly hardening. Wax always felt so nice going on, Jackie thought, and so bad coming off. Her eyes began to water in anticipation.

·Replacement Theory·

The last time I saw Janice she was standing on the lawn in front of the house. The kid, Bryant, was crawling around in the grass, pausing every so often to sit back on his knees and shriek at the moving van. "Twuck! Twuck!" He was eighteen months and still not walking, a source of great worry and embarrassment for Janice. The doctor she'd brought him to didn't think it was a problem. He assured her that the child would, someday, get off his hands and knees. It wouldn't have been such a big deal except that Bryant was unusually tall, more the size of an average three-year-old, and so the sight of him moving around on all fours, like a baby, was unsettling.

I was on my way to pick up Oscar from school, and was embarrassed when she spotted me across the street.

Janice was dressed that day the way she always dressed, as if she was about to go on a cruise, in white jeans, a bright gauzy top, low-heeled sandals, her hair a mop of black curls. She had lost a lot of weight and looked better than ever, the way divorcing women so often do — one of life's tiny justices.

Janice watched the moving men come in and out of the house carrying boxes, and she looked almost amused, as if this was funny, what was happening to her right now — the unraveling of her life. Her husband, Greg, was already living with the new woman and Janice and the kid were moving out of town, starting over on the East Coast. Rodney and I had been looking for a house for over a year, the whole time we were friends with them. We'd turned up our noses at one place after another. When we learned that they were breaking up and putting their house on the market, we both had the same thought: This was the house we'd been waiting for. It seemed almost serendipitous the way the timing worked out.

Still, when she waved, I felt caught somehow, like a vulture circling its prey.

"I'm almost finished here," she said with a short laugh. "You can get the key from Greg tomorrow."

"No rush," I said. "I mean, I wasn't coming to see if you were gone. I was just on my way to get Oscar from school." I nodded my head up the block. It was the same toddler program Bryant had been scheduled to start in the fall. You practically had to apply at birth to get your child in. When Janice had canceled, a spot had opened up for Oscar. Now Bryant would be going somewhere else, a Montessori in Washington, D.C.

The moving men came past now carrying a giant mirror. It was hidden inside padded blankets, but I could tell what it was from the size and shape. I remembered it had been propped in the entryway to the house. I remembered liking it, the bold narcissism of it sitting there, taking up all that wall space, instead of art. Janice mentioned she might be leaving a few things, belongings too cumbersome to drag across the country, but this apparently wasn't one of them. I watched, disappointed, as it disappeared inside the truck.

The house was much bigger than the apartment where we'd been living—and the furniture we owned wasn't as nice as theirs. I was the first to admit it.

Beside me, Janice sighed. "It hit me this weekend," she said, crossing her arms. "It's really over."

"I'm so sorry," I said. "About everything."

She gave me that short laugh again. "Well, at least something good has come out of it. At least you guys are getting a nice house."

"Yeah, well . . ." I said, but let the words drift off.

"I told Greg last night, 'You discard people.' I told him, 'You treat people like things.' He agreed. I feel sorry for the new woman. I really do. He's going to do the same thing to her. Just wait and see."

"I'm sure you're right. God, what a jerk," I said, but my mind was up the street, on Oscar. I couldn't linger here, chatting, if I was going to be on time. But it seemed rude to breeze off.

The moving men came out carrying pieces of the bed frame. Janice watched them and laughed again, a raspy sound this time. "What was I thinking? That's what I keep asking myself. Shouldn't I have sensed he had a problem before I went off and married him? Had a kid with him?"

"No, you couldn't have known," I muttered, staring up the block toward the school. It was starting to seem like a long conversation.

"He's addicted to new relationships. He thrives on that shit, the gifts, the thrilling sex, the six-hour-fucking-getting-to-know-you phone calls. He only likes the beginnings of stories. He likes to be the hero."

"That's not good," I said, though really I was thinking it sounded fun, all that stuff that came with beginnings.

"So stupid of me," Janice went on. "My mother told me. She said, 'Whatever you do, don't marry a black man.'" Janice glanced at me after she said it, I guess checking to see how it might sit with me. "I know, I know," she said. "I shouldn't say things like that. It's not nice. But it's true. Black men can't be trusted. That's just a fact. I never even dated one before Greg."

I didn't know what to say, so I just nodded. I was really eager to go now.

But she wasn't finished. She fingered her curls as she spoke about a psychic she'd seen in Venice. "He told me the next man I'm going to meet is going to be a single parent. Somebody blond. Somebody into yoga. He told me to hang around in school yards and yoga studios."

"That sounds great. Listen, I'd really better get going."

We stood for a moment, silence filling the air between us. Off to the side, I could see Bryant crawling across the porch, getting under the feet of the moving men.

I hugged Janice stiffly, thanking her for the recent helpful e-mails about the alarm system, the satellite dish, the Internet provider. We promised to keep in touch. She said she would shoot me an e-mail when she got to D.C.

As I started away, I thought about what she'd said about black men. And I thought about how I hadn't even known Greg was black for the longest time. He was tall, with wavy brown hair and pale skin, sharp features, and he always seemed to be grinning, his large teeth and gums exposed. I thought she was the black one and that they were an interracial couple. After I found out (somehow it came up in casual conversation) I could sort of see it, but it was funny how long I'd gone seeing them as something they weren't.

Halfway up the block, I turned back once more to wave good-bye, but she wasn't looking at me. She was holding both of Bryant's hands and trying to force him to walk, but his legs dangled like wet noodles, and he was laughing with his head tilted up to the sky.

Our moving day came and Janice was gone. Not a sign of her and Greg was left in the house, not a single roll of toilet paper. I stood in the center of the empty living room, thinking how I could have never imagined living in a house like this back when I was poor and single.

I'd lived in squalor for most of my twenties, in apartments with roaches and bad carpeting, sleeping on a mattress on the floor with a milk crate turned upside down as my nightstand. I'd subsisted on Chinese takeout, ramen noodles, black beans and rice. I had not known comfort until I met Rodney.

I was thirty-four at the time and had just ended another two-year relationship. I'd had a whole string of them—they all ended at two years, like an expiration date, a string of willowy boys in grungy jeans who split the bill down the middle at restaurants and went to therapy and had been forbidden to play with guns as children.

Rodney was different. He was older than me by fifteen years, and richer than me—a real adult man with a mortgage and a secretary and cuff links and shiny black shoes. He gave no thought to using valet parking and only flew business class. He was an attorney. A long time ago he'd been a public defender but now he only took on private clients. I'd met him one night at a wine bar where I was out with a girlfriend. I noticed him immediately, sitting alone in his suit, tie pulled loose. He caught me looking and bought me a drink from across the room, just like the men do in television movies. My friend made herself scarce and I joined him at his table. We talked about his work and ultimately about his marriage. The ring was hard not to notice—it was thick platinum and glinted in the candlelight. He told me it was over. They still lived together, still slept in the same bed, but didn't have sex anymore. He wanted to leave her but he didn't know how. They'd been trying to have a baby for years and had been unable to. Every time his wife got pregnant—it had happened five times—she miscarried. The last one had been the worst. She'd carried the child for eighteen weeks. They had learned it was a boy already, and had named him Noah. They went on a weekend trip to Santa Barbara to celebrate their first time reaching the second trimester. They were out shopping for clothes at a fancy maternity shop called Due when Rodney heard an animal groan from the dressing room. He knew what it was and put his face in his hands and just sat there waiting for her to emerge.

We began meeting secretly for wine at this bar. I learned only his wife's name—Linda—and that they had gone to law school together. He told me they were miserable together but that it would look bad if he left her now—as if he was leaving her because she had failed to make him a baby.

I told him something I remembered from a meditation class I'd taken years before. What matters is your intention. If your intention is pure, then you can be sure you are doing the right thing. "As long as you're leaving her in the right spirit," I told him, "it doesn't matter what she chooses to think. You can't control that."

After he ended things with her, we never heard from Linda again. Turns out that when there are no children, divorces are clean. There is no reason to ever speak again.

Rodney was not a man who liked to be alone. My friend, the

one who had been beside me at the bar the night I met him, told me, "Men are like monkeys swinging through a jungle. They don't let go of the vine until they've already gotten a grip on the next one." I was only thirty-four but I was frightened if I waited too long—if I was too picky—I would wake up one day and discover it was too late. I didn't yet have a career but I wanted a home more. Overnight I went from living like a squatter to bourgeois comfort. Rodney's bachelor pad—small but plush, with shining stainless-steel appliances—was the fanciest place I'd ever lived. When he was at work, I would walk around the house stroking things, lying in the giant bed, feeling like an immigrant maid at her first job in America.

We moved quickly: six months of getting-to-know-you before I got pregnant. I was relieved at how simple the roles were: Rodney was the breadwinner. I would make the babies. We watched the baby grow inside me with shared joy and awe. But sometimes I thought I saw a glint of sadness cross Rodney's face when we walked out of yet another triumphant doctor's appointment. I wondered if he was thinking about the other wife, the other baby boy.

Now I stared at him where he stood on the sidewalk outside Janice and Greg's house, ours now, holding Oscar on his shoulders. They were watching the men trying to park the moving van in front of the house. This was the first home we would own together. It was big and beautiful and American, with more cabinet and closet space than I had ever dreamed of.

The street around them looked like a movie set for a film

about the fifties. Just up the block was a large white house that Janice once told me was the actual place they filmed *Happy Days*. Our house too looked like that to me, a pre-everything house. Standing at the window, I felt for a moment my luck. I had the man, the child, the house. I said out loud, "I'm happy. I'm as happy as I've ever been." In the cleared-out room, my voice was startling, and I looked around to see if anybody had heard me.

In bed that night, Rodney sat propped up against pillows beside me, scribbling notes about the trial he was working on. Another rich man was being accused of murder. I could see black-and-white photographs—a woman's body splayed on the ground, her skirt hiked up.

I turned to my side, away from the image. We hadn't had sex in weeks and I knew we wouldn't tonight. We were both too tired. There was the move, of course, and then there was Oscar. He had been having night terrors for many weeks now, and it had killed any remaining desire we felt toward one another. One of us was in the room with him at least twice a night, trying to wake him out of his shrieking fits. He looked awake but he screamed as if he was being bludgeoned. He could not be woken from the dream. You just had to hold him until he slowly fell back to sleep.

I looked around the room. The last time I'd been in this room there had been a different bed in this spot—a tall, dramatic sleigh bed all dressed in white bedding. Janice kept a fresh bunch of roses on their dresser in a glass bowl. The book on their nightstand had been, I recalled, a bestseller, a pop sociology book whose title I could not remember anymore.

Janice had led me through this room to the backyard, where she'd smoked and told me for the first time about the problems she and Greg were having. It was all just beginning to unravel then. She said he'd been traveling a lot lately and that the previous Sunday morning she'd been up early in the living room, playing with Bryant, when she heard a blooping sound on his cell phone, a text message coming in.

"A red flag went up," she said. "I mean, you don't get text messages early on Sunday morning from work or from a friend." She went to the phone and picked it up and saw the words on the screen. *My body is screaming out for you. Call.* The writer had signed it with an S, "like a snake slithering across the screen," Janice said.

When she confronted Greg, he quickly admitted to the affair. He told her that the thrill was gone from their marriage, ever since she had gotten pregnant. He said he knew it was his fault. He didn't find motherhood sexy. He didn't touch Janice very often, and when he did, he felt like they were going through the motions. He averted his eyes from her when she got undressed in front of him. She had to suck him with her mouth to get him hard enough to enter her, she told me, otherwise he remained soft, like a newborn baby.

She said all of this to me with a weirdly encouraging smile, as if she was giving me permission to burst into laughter.

I didn't laugh, though I think I might have smiled while she spoke, only because she was smiling and my face automatically returned the expression.

"But we're going to work it out," Janice had told me, sitting just feet from where I lay now, in my own bed. "We just need some time to nurture the relationship—to remember why we chose each other in the first place."

I remember thinking it sounded like something she had read in a book.

I turned to Rodney now, to say something about Janice, about how sad it all was that things had ended the way they had. But he was asleep already, the work file lying on the nightstand beside him.

I didn't sleep well beside Rodney in our new bedroom, surrounded by all those unpacked boxes. The room felt too cold and so I turned on the heat but then it felt too hot so I turned it off. When I was finally drifting off to sleep at three in the morning, I was awoken by screaming. Oscar. I clambered out of bed and stumbled through the maze of boxes to his room. I found him standing up in his crib. His eyes were open and he was screaming, "*Mommy, Mommy*," but when I went and stood in front of him, he kept screaming. I picked him up and carried him, thrashing, to the rocking chair in the corner. I held him and rocked him, saying, "Mommy's here, Mommy's here," over and over, but he kept shrieking and looking around the darkness wildly, as if he were searching for somebody else. The sound of his weeping was so sad that I began to cry myself. And then, abruptly, he dropped into a deep sleep on my lap, as if he'd never cried at all.

———— ◆ ————

I was on my way back from my morning power walk a few days later, dressed in spandex and sneakers, when I saw a BMW parked in our driveway. It was a convertible sports model, with an Obama sticker on the fender. The election had come and gone, the blackish man was in charge, and the slogan on the bumper—*Yes We Can*—already had the feeling of some dusty, long-gone revolution.

I recognized it as Greg's car. One of Janice's many complaints about Greg was that after they'd had a child he insisted on making choices that suggested he was still single, like this tiny car. As I neared the house, I heard the sound of men's laughter floating out the window. Through the glass, I could make out Greg seated next to Rodney on the couch. They were laughing about something but all I could make out were the words "the end of kissing." I entered the house quietly and for a moment it was like they didn't see me. I only caught the end of Greg's sentence, "woodworking in a basement."

They both looked up at me, still smirking, their eyes afire with some private male joke.

"It's the lady of the house!" Greg said. Everything he said sounded like it had an exclamation point attached to it. "I hear you like the new digs!"

"The house is beautiful. We love it."

His teeth gleamed, white and straight, like a German army in his mouth. His eyes flickered up and down my body with what looked like amusement.

"Jogging?"

"Power walking," I said, self-conscious now, wishing I'd worn a longer shirt.

Just then, a woman's soft voice spoke, as if from the ether. "You must be Tracy."

I turned around. She stood—delicate, exquisite—in our hallway, drying her hands on a paper towel. "I didn't mean to frighten you," she said. For a moment I was confused enough to think maybe it was Janice standing before me. It didn't really look like her, but there were some similarities—the black ringlet hair, the light brown skin, and the prominent teeth.

"I'm Soleil," she said, moving toward me, a hand outstretched, a slight, tentative smile on her face.

I couldn't tell from looking at her where she came from. Her features were a confusion of races, a new world order on her face. She was dressed like a rich Buddhist, pure California in a fringed white scarf, loose flowing clothes, rows of brown and orange prayer beads on her wrist.

I felt huge and lumbering beside her. I shook her hand,

which was still moist from washing, then watched as she floated over to the couch and sat next to Greg.

"She's tiny," Janice had told me about the other woman. "Greg likes thin women with no asses." She'd also said, "She's black, or mixed, or something. He only dates women with color." At the time, I remember noticing this phrasing—"women with color"—and wondering if she'd really meant "women of color"—because I knew from college, all the protest and identity hysteria, that these were not the same thing. You could be a woman *with* color who wasn't *of* color. Or vice versa. Anyway, Janice said it all in the same droll voice, wearing the same bemused smile.

"Greg came to pick up his mail," Rodney said from the couch. "And to introduce us to Soleil. They just got a place together in Venice. They said we should come visit one of these days."

I looked from Rodney to Greg to Soleil, three smiling faces, wondering how I should respond to this.

"The air is great there for children," Greg said. "And we're near the beach."

"Where is your little one?" Soleil asked.

"At school," I said, but then remembered it was Saturday. He wasn't at school. Fear rinsed over me. Where was he? Where had I left him?

"He's not at school," Rodney said, with a laugh. "Remember? Betty came and took him to a playdate this morning."

Betty was the sitter who sometimes worked for us on weekends. I forced a laugh. "Oh, right," I said.

They were all staring at me, now not smiling.

"Excuse me," I said, and went to the kitchen to get a glass of water. I could hear them in the other room, discussing the new house Greg and Soleil had moved into. They were renting it from an actress who had been somewhat famous in the eighties. She had been the lead in several thrillers. I remembered her face. She had pale skin and dark hair and sad eyes. I hadn't thought about her in a while, and stood listening from the kitchen as they talked about her.

"She never really came to anything," Greg was saying. "I'm not sure why she fizzled."

"I heard she became a Scientologist," Soleil said.

"Before or after she stopped getting roles?"

"After."

"Trying to E-meter her way back to the big time, huh?" Rodney said. "That never works. I've tried it."

"You were a Scientologist?" Soleil asked.

Greg laughed. "Rodney, I'd like to introduce you to the most gullible woman you'll ever meet. He was kidding, babe."

"No, I was being serious," Rodney said. "I was a member of the church when I was younger."

"Yeah, right."

Rodney said, "It's true!"

I couldn't tell if Rodney was being serious, and waited, not breathing, to hear what else he'd say. Maybe he had been a Scientologist. It seemed possible. But everything was quiet in the other room, and when I peeked in I saw that Soleil was on Greg's lap, fingering his hair. Rodney was leaning back on the sofa with his arm slung over the back, watching them, a faint smile on his lips.

I knew I should go and join them, it was only polite, but I wanted to be alone instead. I went down the hall to the bedroom.

I sat at the edge of the bed, unlacing my sneakers. Then I lay back against the comforter and stared at the ceiling fan, where it spun in slow circles, letting off a faint breeze. I could hear the voices of the men down the hall, low and inscrutable.

I thought about Oscar. I missed him with a terrible hunger. The first time they handed him to me in the hospital bed, I looked at his face and thought to myself, *And then they lived happily ever after*, as if the story were about somebody else. Oscar was to me the perfect model upon which all other babies were based. And yet, even then, it seemed precarious.

I heard somebody breathing in the room with me and turned my head to the side.

It was Soleil. She stood in the entryway to the bedroom. "Sorry to interrupt. The men sent me to find you."

I sat up. "Oh, sorry. I was tired."

She stepped inside, her arms crossed. "I hope this isn't uncomfortable for you."

"No, no."

"I understand you were close to Janice. Greg tells me you were her best friend while she was here. You were the one thing she regretted about leaving this town. Having made a friend like you."

"Oh, well, yeah," I said, but I wasn't sure it was true. Had we been that close? We saw a lot of each other for a while, then we didn't see each other.

I rose to my feet.

Soleil stood in the middle of the room, looking around, her expression half somber, half excited. I tried to imagine what she was seeing: This was where Janice and Greg had made a baby. This was also where their marriage had gone bad, where Soleil's future had become a possibility.

Janice had told me many times the story of how Soleil entered their lives. She would tell it to me each time as if it were the first and I'd nod and act indignantly shocked each time. At first Soleil had just been a casual acquaintance of both Janice and Greg, somebody they met through mutual friends and saw at parties now and then. Soleil had been single, childless, mid to late thirties, desperate for a grown-up life of her own. You could sniff it on her—the way you could on some women—the hunger for a man, a baby, the intention to have it all by any means necessary. A woman who has clung to her freedom too long and grown tired of it, but who might be stuck with this freedom for the rest of her life if she doesn't play her cards right. "I felt sorry for her," Janice told me. "Can you believe that? I thought she seemed lonely and felt bad for her."

Now, standing before me in the bedroom, Soleil spoke quickly, in a half whisper. "I'm sure she told you I stole him, but the thing is, the marriage was already broken. I mean, Greg was dying in there. I wish things had gone differently, but I love Greg. And I know she's your friend, but I know for a fact he never loved her. And she didn't love him either."

I didn't know what to say, so I just said, "Well, it's hard to say what goes on between two people. From the outside."

Up close, I could see that Soleil had probably not been so pretty at some point. She'd figured out a way to disguise what was slightly ferretlike about her features—to make them work for her.

Her hair was working for her. I'd always wanted curly hair, like Jennifer Beals or Chaka Khan. When I was in high school I used to get my hair permed every six weeks so that nobody knew I didn't really have curly hair. I was prettier with curly hair, my features more interesting, but I'd stopped perming it in college because it was getting brittle. I'd accepted what nature gave me, but looking at Soleil, I felt that old hunger again to look exotic and unclassifiable.

"Please don't hate me," Soleil said.

"I don't even know you."

I had intended it to sound cold, a rejection, but she took it as the opposite, an invitation.

"Thank you," she said, smiling. "For not judging me. Greg said you were a kind person, a compassionate person. He said you would give me a chance."

I could hear the men's voices moving toward us down the hall. "Ladies, ladies," Greg was calling. "Are you two up to no good?"

———◆———

After Soleil and Greg were gone, I stared out the window, waiting for Oscar and Betty to come back.

Behind me, Rodney said, "She's interesting. I like her."

"She looks like Janice," I said. "For a second I thought it was her."

Rodney chuckled. "You're joking, right?"

I turned around, shook my head.

"She doesn't look a thing like Janice," he said. "I can't imagine two women who look less alike."

I was about to ask him what he meant, but I heard Oscar's voice on the street outside and turned to see him, chunky and golden, running up the walkway toward the house, Betty behind him with the stroller. I went out to greet him. He leaped into my arms and I held him, inhaling the smells from the park, the car exhaust and the pollen mixed together in his hair.

———◆———

That night in bed I woke to the sound of screaming. It was once again three in the morning. Rodney whispered into the darkness, "Leave him. Let him work it out." I lay there watching the clock, but the numbers weren't moving fast enough. Oscar sounded different this time too, like something was really the matter. "Momma, Momma," he wept. My throat went dry and my palms got wet. Finally, ten minutes into it, I said, "I'm sorry, I can't stand it."

Rodney sighed as I slid out of bed, and said, "This is why you're tired all the time. This is why you're only half here."

When I picked Oscar up, he was soaking with sweat. His body was stiff and did not relax into my embrace. He kicked and shrieked and tried to push himself out of my arms. "Momma, Momma," he wailed, searching the room wildly for somebody else. I finally put him back in the crib, where he continued to shriek and flail around. I backed out of the room. I didn't return to bed but sat in the hallway on the floor hugging my knees, listening as Oscar continued to call, "Momma." After what seemed ages, he went quiet. I got up and went back to bed, where I lay stiffly beside Rodney, not falling back to sleep until the first light of morning.

• ◆ •

The next night when Oscar woke again, screaming, Rodney grabbed my arm before I could go to him. "Stop."

"But listen," I said, my feet already on the floor.

"Momma, Momma!" came Oscar's voice, between guttural sobs.

"Give him fifteen minutes," Rodney said.

"I can't. I just can't."

"You realize you're training him to wake up screaming. If

you go in there, he'll do it again tomorrow night, and the next, and he'll never learn to sleep through the night. He'll be tired all the time too."

"Momma! Momma!"

I turned and looked at Rodney through the darkness. "But he's just a baby."

"He's two. He's got to learn."

"How long has it been?"

"One minute."

I'd seen a movie once, many years earlier, about a wealthy couple who ignore their young daughter's cries while they make love. Down the hall, she is being kidnapped. But this time I waited it out.

When the weeping finally stopped, Rodney said, "Eight minutes. It took all of eight minutes."

———◦◆◦———

Wednesday night—date night—Rodney and I drove west on the 10 to meet Soleil and Greg for dinner. I hadn't thought we'd ever see them again, but here we were.

Oscar had not wanted to be left behind with Betty tonight. She hadn't been able to distract him with finger puppets as we were leaving the way she usually did. She had to physically restrain him, and he thrashed and wept as if we were sending him to the gas chamber. The sound of his wailing was still echoing in my bones as we drove along the crowded freeway.

Rodney had organized the dinner behind my back. He'd sprung it on me just before Betty was due to arrive, as if it was the thing I'd always wanted, a date night with Greg and Soleil.

"I have a surprise for you," he'd said, smiling at himself in the mirror as he buttoned up his linen shirt. "Guess what we're doing tonight?"

"What?"

"We're going to dinner with Greg and Soleil."

"Wait a minute," I said. "How do you think Janice would feel if she knew we were hanging out with them? I mean, coming to get the mail is one thing, but—"

"Janice is gone," he'd said, examining his nose in the mirror. He glanced back at me and shrugged. "Anyway, you never really liked Janice. She was a bore. You said so."

"I never said that."

"Yes, you did. I remember your words. You said, 'Every time she opens her mouth I get sleepy.'"

I didn't remember saying anything like that. I didn't remember feeling it either, but I couldn't be sure.

"She wasn't boring," I said, then repeated it for emphasis. "She *wasn't* boring."

"Name one interesting thing about her," Rodney said, turning to face me. "She said she was going to design handbags but she never did. Then she wanted to become an events planner. That was her goal. Events planning. I'm sorry, but if Greg didn't want to stay trapped in a Lifetime movie, more power to him."

I'd never thought Rodney paid that much attention to Janice, but he remembered more details about her than I did.

"Why are we even discussing this?" I said.

He shrugged, turned back to the mirror, and began adjusting his slacks. "I just don't want you to be so judging. We're all adults here. Let's have a nice evening."

———◆———

They were waiting for us outside the restaurant.

Soleil was wearing something that looked like red satin pajamas. She came toward me and hugged me tightly before I could stop her. "You look beautiful," she said. "I love that color blue on you." I could feel her body, bony and lithe, the body I'd always wanted, beneath the pajamas. She smelled like a church. Greg hovered beside her, waiting for his turn to hug me.

"I'm so happy you decided to join us!" he said, gripping my arms and staring at me in the eyes before he embraced me.

Over dinner, Rodney asked Soleil questions about herself. She told us she was a healer. She practiced Reiki and taught yoga twice a week at a local studio. She was studying to become a "spiritual counselor" at some New Age center with a pseudo-African name. She was writing a screenplay too, a magic realism coming-of-age story based on her childhood in Nevada.

I looked across the table at Rodney, waiting to see the sarcastic smirk on his face. He liked to say about L.A., "Everybody wants to be a fucking guru." But he was watching Soleil talk, nodding, totally serious. And when she was done telling us about her work, Rodney said to her, "You should teach Tracy yoga. She needs to relax."

I listened, wondering about Janice and Bryant, what they were doing in D.C., where it was snowing.

During the main course, I asked, "How's Bryant adjusting to his new life?"

Greg's face stiffened slightly at the mention of his son, but he recovered with his enormous grin. "He's great. Just fantastic. He's in this amazing new school. Montessori. Their Toddler Twos program. Super-high-tech."

He started telling us how they had a video camera in all the classrooms, and you could log in on their Web site to watch, in real time, your child playing throughout the day. "Like a surveillance camera," he said.

"Is that strange," I said, "watching him through a computer screen?"

Greg paused. "I haven't actually tried it yet."

I nodded and looked into my water, trying to picture Bryant through a video surveillance camera, the kind that makes everything look seedy and criminal, imagined him tiny and distant and grainy, crawling across a classroom. I wondered if he'd ever learned to walk.

———— • ◆ • ————

In the parking lot, Soleil hugged me again, tighter this time. She said, "I'm so glad you decided to come, Tracy." She asked if we could have coffee next week, just the two of us. She said she would give me a private yoga class if I liked.

I hesitated, thinking distantly of Janice, but I couldn't remember her very well now. I remembered other details about her, things she'd said, details she'd told me, intimate and sad, about her and Greg. Other things too—the slight bemused smile she wore all the time, always planted on her face, whether she was talking about something sad or something happy— how disconcerting I found that smile. And I remembered her outfits—the white jeans and the flowing brightly colored tops and her hair, a coil of black curls. I even remembered that her toenails were always painted a muted shade of burgundy, long toes peeking out from her strappy low-heeled sandals. But I couldn't remember her face, only all the context around that face, facts and figures, colors and sounds, but not the face itself.

It was like a sad dream you wake from feeling intensely, as if it really happened, but within moments the details of it have evaporated, leaving the feeling of grief but not the reason for it.

"Can we do that, Trace?" Soleil was saying. She was all lit up by the streetlight, ethereal, with her sepia skin and her shiny black curls, the exotic beauty I'd always hoped to become.

Behind her the two men stood, pretending to talk to each

other, but I could see their eyes were on us. They were waiting to see what I'd say, if I'd join Soleil for lunch, a yoga class. Waiting to see if I'd be her friend.

"Sure," I said, my mouth dry, hollow, airy as the dead now. "Let's do that."

———— •◆• ————

We drove home on the freeway, the hills a dark shadow hovering in the distance beneath a cloud of smoke. You couldn't really tell at night, but there were fires raging in those hills, the way they did every year, devouring the living and the dead. If you breathed in too deeply, it hurt your lungs.

Rodney spoke beside me. "Soleil's nice, isn't she? I mean, interesting."

"I guess so."

"I have a feeling you two are gonna hit it off," he said, and he reached over and squeezed my knee.

I was quiet, thinking about Janice again. I tried to remember her face, but it was disappearing now. It was almost gone.

"What did she look like?"

"Who?"

"Janice. What did she look like?"

Rodney glanced at me. "Don't you remember?"

I shook my head. "Not really."

"I'm not surprised."

I didn't ask him what he meant. Instead I looked out the window beside me and tried to see my own reflection there in the dark glass, but all I could see was what was behind it, the other cars moving past, and beyond them, distantly, a stucco housing development. I rolled down the window and let some of the outside air blow in on me.

"Could you shut that?" I heard Rodney say, as if from a great distance. "I'm cold."

But I left it open, my eyes closed, letting the burning air fill my lungs as we moved east across the city.

·There, There·

I see the headline after lunch.

It's on the Internet—a newswire report about something that happened just this morning. TIME MAGAZINE EDITOR DIES IN FALL.

My boyfriend is an editor at *Time* magazine, so I can't help but feel a tightening in my throat as I click on the headline.

The article opens and I am relieved to see that it was a business editor—somebody in a totally different department from my boyfriend. A forty-two-year-old business editor who wrote an occasional advice column on personal investing. He is survived by his wife, Deborah, who is a business writer for a different magazine. The police suspect suicide. He jumped at ten a.m. from the fifteenth floor of the *Time* magazine offices, which the article says is the highest floor in the building. I am surprised by this detail. I have been inside the lobby of this building and somehow imagined it to be a lot taller than fifteen stories. Maybe a hundred and fifteen. He landed on the roof of a garage next to the building.

When I'm done reading, I call my boyfriend at his office. Even though I already know it wasn't he who jumped, I'm happy when I hear his voice. He sounds harried.

"What's up?" he says. I can hear his fingers tapping away on the keyboard in the background.

"Nothing," I say. "I was just calling because—"

I hesitate. I decide to let him bring it up.

"Just calling to say hi," I say.

"Hi," he says. "How was lunch?"

"Pretty good." I tell him about my lunch, the noodle shop I went to, the guy at the table across from mine who ordered the same thing I did, how I pretended not to notice and avoided his eyes. But I can tell I'm babbling and I can tell he is distracted.

"Really," he says.

"Really," I say. "So what's going on over there?"

"Nothing," he says. "I'm just pressed for time. Sorry. I have to close this article in the next hour."

"No, don't worry about it."

After I say it, I realize I'm nervous. I really want him to tell me about the man who fell.

But the next thing he says is, "Are we still meeting later?"

"Yes, for bibimbap."

I wait a beat, give him one more chance.

But he doesn't say it. He just says in a clipped voice, "Listen, I gotta run. Can we talk later?"

I am sweating now. "Okay, bye."

"Bye," he says, and hangs up.

———◆———

My roommate is home—the one who never uses the kitchen, the one who seems to be disappearing. She might be in her forties, but it's possible she is much younger. She looks both very old and very young, like a stooped grandmother and a pre-pubescent girl. It's hard to tell with somebody who doesn't eat, because the bones show through the skin. It is surprising to me every time I see her. I think it's not possible to get any thinner, and then she gets thinner.

I go to her room and stand in the doorway, watching as she rifles through a drawer.

She is only half dressed in a red skirt and a black lacy bra. All the vertebrae in her back are visible when she leans forward.

"Can I ask you something?"

She looks up and smiles.

"Yes," she says. "Ask me something."

"Do you think this is strange?" I go on then and tell her what happened, the article I read on the Internet, the conversation I had with my boyfriend afterward. "What do you think it means?"

"That's old-school," she says. "To go to work and jump out a window. I didn't know people did that anymore." She finds what she was looking for in the drawer, a pair of scissors, and slices through the air as if cutting an invisible cloth.

"But don't you think it's strange he didn't tell me?"

"Yeah, that's weird too. Maybe he doesn't know about it yet."

"Impossible," I say. "A colleague jumping out a window? A colleague with the same job title? It's in the newswires already. He knows. He's just not saying anything." I pause, cross my arms, then ask, "If somebody jumped out the window of your office, wouldn't you call your boyfriend?"

"I don't have a boyfriend."

"But you know what I mean. If you had one."

"Yeah, I'd call him," she says, smiling strangely for a moment, as if imagining the kind of boyfriend she might have in such a scenario. "I'd call him the second I found out. But that's just me."

She starts applying her makeup in front of this little mirror with lights on either side. There's a lever at the bottom where you can adjust the lights to different "settings": Natural, Office, Evening, Disco. She has it on Disco. She always has it on Disco. She's applying the makeup very carefully. On her boom box she's playing a song from the eighties, Kim Carnes's "Bette Davis Eyes." She hums along as she works on her eyes.

I can see she isn't interested anymore, that she's distracted. "Maybe he was just busy," I say, more to myself, then leave her alone with her mirror.

That night I meet my boyfriend at a Korean restaurant. He is sitting at the table already, reading an article in the *Wall Street Journal*. He is wearing the same thing he wears to work every day. Literally every day. A white button-down shirt and khaki slacks. He has lots and lots of each hanging in his closet. Nothing else.

When I sit down across from him, he tells me about the article he's just finished reading. It's about how food products are often misnamed to make them sound better than they are.

"Like Key lime pie," he says. "It is never really made from Key limes, because they cost too much to import. It's really just made of ordinary limes. Or Chilean sea bass. It's not even related to bass. It's actually called a toothfish."

I nod, then pick up my napkin, unfold it, try to sound casual. "So what happened at work today?"

He shrugs, looks away briefly out the window, as if he's considering something, and then says, "I finished editing the cover story on pesticides. It's done." He holds up his water glass in the air and says, "Hear, hear. To completion."

I clink my glass against his and say, quietly, "Hear, hear." We both take sips.

The waitress comes to the table and he orders bibimbap with beef and I order it with tofu and then he asks me if I wrote anything today.

It's a bad question for him to ask.

I am supposed to be writing a second novel. A long time ago I wrote a first novel. It was golden. The girl in it was easy to like.

The book brought people together. Everyone agreed on its merits. Now they—we—are waiting to see if it was a fluke, if I can do that again. I've been trying to finish the follow-up for almost four years. Actually, it's more complicated than that. I did write a second novel several years ago and even submitted it for publication. But my editor said it was dark, depressing. My agent hated it too. He said there was "nothing redemptive" in it to make anybody care.

Now I am supposedly reworking it, trying to make the main character more sympathetic, but I'm not doing a very good job. Every time the opportunity presents itself to make the character's humanity shine through, I make her do something awful or say something cruel instead. I've already spent the money they gave me to write it. My boyfriend is paying for dinner.

I shrug. "No. Mostly I just read news reports on the Internet."

"All day?" he says. "That's what you did all day?"

"No," I say. "Just part of the day. I got distracted by the news. You know, real stories about real lives."

After I say it I search his face.

"Hmm," he says, frowning. "When do you plan to send a draft to your editor?"

"When I'm finished making it redemptive, I guess," I say, and look away out the window. On the sidewalk a man is leaning against a car with his shirt up while his girlfriend inspects something on his back.

When I look back, my boyfriend is looking at me a little sadly, like he feels sorry for me.

The bibimbap comes in big steaming bowls and we eat it and talk about everything except the editor who jumped. He doesn't mention it, no matter how many times I steer the conversation back to his day at work.

When we are finished eating and paying the bill, he stands up and says, "I'm excited to go to sleep."

We leave the restaurant and he links his arm in mine as we walk back toward his building.

On the way, we pass a newsstand. From a few feet away I can see the late edition of the *Post*. The headline screams out, TIME EDITOR IN DEATH PLUNGE over a photograph of the building itself, with a little black arrow pointing to the window the man jumped from and a little dotted line showing the arc of his descent onto the parking garage twelve stories below.

I pull him to a stop in front of the paper so that there is no way he can miss it. From the corner of my eye, I watch his face. His eyes seem to rest for a beat on the cover of the *Post* but then, abruptly, he reaches forward and picks up a different newspaper, two racks away, the wide flat pink one. He skims the front page, smiles at something, then replaces it on the stand.

"Shall we?" he says.

He pulls me forward, toward his apartment.

———— • ◆ • ————

The second book, the one I already wrote but that they won't accept, poured out of me like something already formed. I wrote it entirely in my pajamas. I rarely left the house during that time except to go to yoga class, where I would simultaneously laugh and weep while lying in corpse pose. Every morning I would drive to the supermarket in my pajamas, where I would purchase my breakfast: a large black coffee and a to-go container of macaroni and cheese. I would consume both in my car in the parking lot with the engine running before driving back home to work more on the book.

At some point I taped the pages of what I'd written all over the walls of my little workspace like wallpaper and paced around, laughing as I read it to myself.

When I handed it in, my editor said, "What is this?"

My agent coughed and said, "Now would be a good moment to explain yourself."

I promised them both I would work on making it more hopeful. I haven't spoken to either of them since.

———◆———

Back at my boyfriend's apartment, I brush my teeth and get undressed and slip into his bed. I lie there with all the lights on, waiting for him as he does his nightly ritual.

Every night it's the same. He checks his e-mail, takes off his white shirt and khaki slacks, does a series of yoga sun salutations, brushes and flosses his teeth, fills up a water bottle, places it on his nightstand, then sets the alarm so that it will play NPR at 6:30 in the morning.

Even his weekends are ritualized. Tomorrow is Saturday and

I know exactly what will happen. We will go to the farmers market at ten a.m. to shop for his week's groceries, and then to a noon movie at the big theater in Union Square, where we will sneak into one more movie than we paid for, and then go back to his apartment, where we will cook an early dinner. Afterward he will leave me at his place while he goes to the gym, where he will do something on a machine while he reads the newspaper or a magazine. After he finishes on the machine, he will come home and go through his night ritual. Maybe we will have sex. Maybe we won't. That's the wild card.

The first time I ever slept at his place, I woke in the morning to the smell of something cooking. I could hear something bubbling on the stove. I saw through the door to the kitchen that he was standing shirtless at the stove, holding a wooden spoon over a big steaming pot.

"What are you making?" I called out to him from the bed.

"Porridge," he called back, without looking up.

Porridge. The word reminded me of a German fairy tale.

He brought it to me in bed, on a tray, in a big steaming bowl. He said it was a family recipe, a Canadian breakfast of champions, and that if I ate it every day I would live a long life. It was gray, like oatmeal, but it was heartier, with beans and seeds and an assortment of grains mixed in. I wasn't sure I liked the taste, but I liked being served it in bed, the steam-fogged window-pane across the room, the blurred and distant world beyond. As I ate the porridge, I understood it was a better breakfast for me than black coffee and macaroni and cheese, and I had the sense that I was finally doing something good and right by being here with him, and that my life was turning a corner.

Now, as he makes tooth-brushing noises in the bathroom, I stare into the brightly lit bedroom. I don't have my glasses on and the room looks grainy and oddly still, like an old color photograph.

I make a list in my head about him. Details I might remember about him someday when he is gone. His skin—the translucent paleness of it. How the first time I lay naked beside him in bed I thought I finally looked dark-skinned next to somebody. How skilled he is at Sunday crossword puzzles, how fast he can finish them, how confused and angry they make me when I try to do them. I think of other things about him too, but in the past tense now: how he never got cold like a normal person—how he could wear T-shirts outside in the winter because, he told me, he had Canadian blood. The time he insisted on playing an old, crackling cassette tape of the "I Have a Dream" speech on Martin Luther King's birthday. How I sat listening beside him on the couch, like a kid in too-tight Sunday school shoes, knees pressed together, hands folded in lap, cheeks burning. And I remember too the time six months ago when we borrowed that little boy, the son of a friend of his, and went for a walk with him in the park. How acutely aware I was that everybody we passed thought the kid was ours. How my boyfriend kept pointing out how cute the kid was, and how I nodded and smiled but secretly didn't think the kid was cute. Sometimes kids aren't cute. Later that day, on the subway ride home, holding hands, he said to me that he liked the names Tristan for a boy and Madeline for a girl. And how it took me a minute to realize he was talking about a baby we might have together. And how surprisd I was to realize he felt our afternoon with the kid had been a success. He thought it brought us closer together, closer to completion. Realizing, not for the first time, that my face didn't actually show what I was thinking.

I suddenly feel sad, like I've already lost something, and when he walks into the room I say out loud, "I'm scared."

"Scared of what?" he says, sliding into bed beside me.

I turn to him and whisper through the darkness, "I don't know. Everything seems so temporary."

He looks at me for a long moment, and I think he's going to say something about what happened this morning, about the man who jumped, but he just kisses me on the forehead and says, "Shush. Let's get some sleep."

Moments later, his eyes are closed and he's snoring.

I lie awake for a long time in the darkness looking at his face as if trying to commit it to memory. In his sleep, his chin goes slack and his face looks irritated, or maybe just bored.

I think about the man who jumped. Did he drink coffee this morning? Did he check his e-mail? Who was on the elevator with him when he went up to the top? Did they chat? Did anybody in the building glance out the window at the exact moment he flew past? When he landed, was there garbage all around him? Were there pigeons? Was there blood, or did he just shatter inside, invisibly?

· The Care of the Self ·

Livy paced the lobby of the hotel, eyeing the Indian arti-facts encased in glass—kachina dolls and squat brown vases, dream catchers and beaded drums. A local pueblo owned the hotel. Engraved in stone above the main entrance were the tribe's words for welcome: *Mah-Waan, Mah-Waan.* Christopher had pointed at the inscription when they came in and said, "My wine, my wine," and now Livy could read it no other way.

From out on the patio she could hear Christopher's voice.

"Where's Dessa?" he kept calling through the air, over and over again. "Has anybody seen Dessa?" Then the inevitable, "There's Dessa! You scared me!" followed by the child's irre-pressible laughter.

Peekaboo. It never failed to amuse the child. At ten months, she still believed that what she could see could not see her. She could not yet walk, but she could hold on to furniture and edge her chubby limbs along with quiet determination. Livy had read all the baby books and learned that Dessa was neither precocious nor delayed. She was in all respects an average ten-month-old, a fact that Livy found oddly comforting.

She checked her watch. Ramona was due to arrive on the airport shuttle any minute. Livy hadn't seen her friend since they both lived in New York. It had only been three years, but in that short interval of time, everything had changed for both of them.

In New York, Ramona had been married to Julian, a music journalist with butterscotch skin and dreadlocks. And Livy had been single, the sidekick girlfriend they had invited over to their Brooklyn apartment for dinner on weekends. Livy would sit in a leather armchair entertaining them with tales of her disastrous dates, and Ramona and Julian would hold hands on their velvet couch and cluck their tongues and laugh at appropriate moments, telling her not to worry, she'd meet somebody, she just had to be patient and focus on making herself whole, because a good relationship was made of two wholes, not two halves.

Livy always left those dinners with Ramona and Julian more distressed than when she'd arrived, nearly bludgeoned by the happiness of their union. She even wondered some nights if the real reason they invited her over was to remind themselves that it was better to be married than to be alone like sad little Livy Thurman.

At the end of the night, Julian would insist on walking her

out to her car, because as Ramona reminded her, a single woman on the street alone was vulnerable. Livy and Julian made awkward small talk once they were alone, and he always insisted on waiting on the curb, shivering in his shirtsleeves, until she'd started the engine and pulled away. She would drive home feeling worse than ever, imagining Julian going back up to the warmth of their apartment, joining his wife on the couch, the two of them drinking red wine and clucking their tongues in pity over her for a while before they retired to their bedroom to make love. She imagined that the specter of her own pathetic figure acted as a kind of aphrodisiac for them. After sex, they would spoon together under the duvet, and invisibly, silently, Julian's sperm would swim at record speed toward Ramona's ripe ovum, colliding to create a golden love child. Ramona had a black father and a Korean-white mother and Julian had a white father and a black mother. This cultural chaos made their union somehow more perfect in Livy's eyes, more natural, more enviable.

Rarely in life could you locate the exact moment when everything changed—when the first domino tipped over—but in this case, it had been sharply, violently marked.

One February night Livy got a call from a weeping, nearly incoherent Ramona. She was in the emergency room, she told Livy through her tears. She had been walking home after work—three blocks from home—when something hard whacked her in the face. She had been confused, dizzy for a moment, and it took her a beat before she realized she was being attacked. Three girls—black girls no older than fifteen, with baby faces and slicked-back ponytails—descended on her with geriatric canes. They went at it, beating her for several minutes, shouting "fucking Rican" and "Dominican whore" and "white bitch"—a confused stream of racial epithets—before an old Jamaican man ran out of a store to stop it. The girls dispersed, whooping and laughing, in all directions. It was, the police told her, a gang initiation. They said somebody was probably videotaping the attack. Ramona had to have sixteen stitches in her forehead. She asked Livy to pick her up because she couldn't reach Julian on his cell phone.

Livy rushed to the hospital and brought the shaking, battered Ramona back to her apartment. She tucked her into bed and sat on the couch waiting for Julian to come home. At some point Livy fell asleep, and when she woke it was morning and Ramona was sitting on the edge of the velvet sofa beside her, weeping. She looked worse than she had in the hospital. Her head had swollen and her face was twisted in anguish. Ramona told Livy this was the third time Julian had disappeared all night. He was with somebody. He had called to tell her he was with a man, someone named Cleavon whom he had met at a bar.

He hadn't heard Ramona's voice mail message and had blurted out his confession before she could tell him what had happened to her.

After the divorce, Ramona threw herself into her work with newfound ambition. She got a job at a law firm in midtown and worked late most nights. On the nights she wasn't working, she was out with other lawyers, drinking in dark glittery bars or eating sushi in restaurants that Livy could not afford.

And Livy? Sad little Livy Thurman flew to Santa Fe one day in February to meet with a gallery owner who was interested in including her work in a group show. She recalled the drive from the airport in Albuquerque, how the dark clouds moving across the sky seemed to ride alongside her rental car like a herd of wild horses. In New York, weather just happened. Here, it announced itself from miles away. As she pulled into Santa Fe, she could see the storm cloud hovering over the distant mountains, could hear rolling thunder. But it had not rained until the afternoon—just in time for her meeting at the gallery. It rained so hard it made the town look blurred at the edges. She sat with the gallery owner, Christopher, in the bright white room looking over her slides, the smell of warmth and damp between them, the steady gray blur of rain outside that made them talk in hushed voices, near whispers, though they were alone.

When all the business talk was done and the rain had ceased, he suggested they go someplace for dinner. Outside, the streets felt empty, as if the crowds of tourists, along with the dust, had been washed away in the downpour. He led her on foot down winding side roads out of town, telling her of his childhood on an Arapaho reservation, of his German-Arapaho mother and his Scottish-Arapaho father, and of his hatred of Santa Fe for its wealth and its white people and its rows of Indian trinket sellers who were, he realized one day, like trinkets themselves. He hated yuppie centers like this, he said, and yet, he admitted, he was unsuited and unwilling to live anywhere else. Years before, he had been plucked from the rez for a scholarship to a prestigious university, and now he was a vegetarian who did yoga. He owned an art gallery. He'd gone all paleface, he said, to the point that he'd never be able to or want to go back to the rez.

He touched the small of her back when they crossed the street.

Now she was living with him under this mood ring of a sky and they had a baby and were thinking of trying for another just as soon as Dessa was weaned and sleeping through the night.

Somewhere in the hotel lobby, Christopher's voice rang out. "Where's Dessa? Has anybody seen Dessa?" And the child's delighted laughter at having eluded him yet again.

The shuttle van arrived. Livy glanced at herself in the large mirror by the revolving doors, trying to see herself through Ramona's eyes, anticipating what she would think of the new Livy. She weighed the same as she had before the baby, but she knew she did not look the same. The pounds had redistributed themselves—smaller ass, bigger belly, full breasts where there once had been none. She had looked like such a New Yorker before, thin, sardonic, with twenty variations of black in her wardrobe. When she dared wear color, it was subtle—or with a hint of irony. She wore high heels a lot back then, black high-heeled boots that left her feet aching. Now she stood in a yellow sundress and comfortable sandals, her once sleek and straightened hair gone back to its ringlet curls and pulled into a messy ponytail that Dessa couldn't yank.

She looked tired. Exhaustion ringed her eyes. Christopher said he found her more beautiful than when he'd first met her that rainy day, but she felt—watching the van pull up to the curb outside—suddenly embarrassed by her lack of style. She wished she'd worn something more sophisticated, something to show Ramona that she had not ceased to care.

And there was Ramona now, getting help from the driver with one hand as she stepped out of the van in low-heeled sandals. With the other hand she held a cell phone, her eyes on the screen. She wore tight blue jeans, a black silky top, her dark curly hair now straight and cut in jagged layers around her face. She looked refreshed for somebody who had just gotten off an airplane.

She came toward Livy smiling, dragging a rolling suitcase behind her.

"Liv, oh my God, what a trip," she said, putting the cell phone in her pocket. "Airplanes are like giant toilets in the sky, don't you think?"

Livy laughed and held out her arms for a hug as it all came back to her, what they'd shared, what they'd liked about each other, who they'd been, how close they'd indeed been, almost like sisters. It was strange. Her new life was so different from the old life that she sometimes felt like a one-woman witness protection program: new man, new baby, new geography, new friends. And she had half convinced herself that the old friendships had not been so deep. But now, at the sight of Ramona's face, she felt relief. Ramona was still the old Ramona, a little harder around the jaw, a little sadder around the eyes, but the same woman she'd loved. And this meant that Livy was still the same Livy, underneath the bright sundress and the western sky.

◦ ◆ ◦

Christopher dragged Ramona's giant suitcase across the gravel to the house while Livy unlatched Dessa from the car seat.

Ramona stood beside her, taking deep hungry breaths of the thin air.

"It's so fucking sweet, Liv, really, to see you happy. And this baby!" She pinched Dessa's cheek and made a loud, harsh kissing sound at the baby's startled face. "Such a chunky monkey. How can you stand it? Don't you just want to eat her up?"

Dessa hid her face in the crook of Livy's neck.

They moved toward the house together, but before they started up the steps, Ramona leaned in to whisper to Livy. "Listen," she said, hanging back. "Is there a health food store anywhere near here?"

Livy laughed. "Are you kidding? This place is lousy with health food."

"Good." Ramona looked over her shoulder to the open door of the house. Christopher had disappeared inside. "Because the thing is, I haven't gone, you know, Number Two, in days. I mean days. It's horrible." She placed a hand on her belly. "I

114

need some help, and naturopaths are great at this kind of thing. This is where they really shine. Can you take me there? I'm desperate."

Dessa squirmed and whined in Livy's arms, tossing her head back like a broken puppet. "Sorry, but I have to put Dessa down for her nap," Livy said. "She has to stay on her schedule."

"Oh, right," Ramona said, glancing at the baby. "Well, just tell me where the Whole Foods is. I'll find it. I'm a New Yorker. I can find my way around anywhere."

Livy gave her directions and the car keys and a moment later stood in a cloud of dust watching Ramona drive off in her car.

Christopher came out into the driveway. "She's intense," he said.

"Good intense or bad intense?"

"Just intense."

———— ◆ ————

On that first meeting, Christopher had looked Puerto Rican to her. Livy had never, as far as she knew, met a real Indian before, had only seen them in television commercials, old men in pigtails, crying. She'd found Christopher immediately, oddly attractive, even if he couldn't dress. He wore an olive-green polo shirt with the collar turned up and stonewashed jeans that had long since gone out of style. He wore his black hair in what was too close to a mullet for comfort.

She had convinced herself when she went to bed with him

that she was just doing it to have one more experience in the world, because that was what she was used to, experiences that led nowhere. Her therapist encouraged such acts, as long as they were safe. She told Livy she was in the information-gathering stage of her life, and that all these short-lived relationships with men were part of her education.

Two Livys fell into Christopher's bed that night—the Watcher and the Doer. The Doer, tipsy and exhilarated with his kisses and the New Mexico sky, could hear the Watcher criticizing Christopher, picking apart his clothes and hair and apartment, his lack of New York edge. She could hear the voice explaining to her that he wasn't good enough for a variety of reasons, but she went through with it anyway and after they'd had sex she fell into a comalike sleep. She woke once in the middle of the night and looked around his room while he slept soundly beside her and felt she was having an affair on herself, could see all of her girlfriends laughing at her, laughing at him, telling her to stop pretending to enjoy herself and get on the plane home. Brooklyn—the only world that mattered—awaited her.

———◆◆———

It was early evening. The two women settled onto the porch with glasses of Zinfandel. Ramona had showered and changed into a sleek black sundress that showed off her figure. She was lean and her arms rippled with muscle. She had the flat stomach of a twenty-year-old.

Livy wore a cardigan and she caught herself leaning forward

to hide her abdomen. "You look so good, Ramona, more beautiful than I've ever seen you."

"Pilates," Ramona said without a pause. "You should try it. None of this yoga crap, where you have to chant in gobbledygook along with some white girl with a nose ring. Pilates is where it's at, girl. No nonsense. You get the most results with the least time spent."

As Ramona talked, Livy took in her friend's face. In New York, people had always taken them for sisters, but they looked nothing alike. Ramona was tall, with wide, athletic shoulders, Livy was short. Ramona had copper skin and slightly Asian eyes, while Livy was pale yellow, with wide, almond-shaped eyes. They shared the same texture hair—half-nappy curls that had been the bane of their equally confused adolescences, which they'd each spent, in different cities, passing as various other races and listening intently to Sade, as if her melancholy British soul held the answer to their alienation. Ramona wore her hair straight and long now, and Livy wore hers curly around her shoulders. Their similarity was not in their features so much as in the relationship between their features: their noses and mouths and eyes came from different continents.

"So what was the whole birth thing like?" Ramona said. "I remember you saying right after that it was long."

Livy looked off into the distance, momentarily at a loss for words. When she turned back to her friend, she could only say, "Yes, long."

Dessa's birth had been a bloody mess—thirty hours of labor,

six hours of active pushing with a New Age doctor who prided himself on his low Cesarean rates. The baby's head had been stuck in the birth canal for hours, but she could not push the child from the purgatory of her body. The problem, they later determined, was that the baby's fist was rigidly held to her cheek, like Rodin's *Thinker*, so that every time Livy pushed, the baby would start to come out, then get pulled back by the spring of her elbow. Finally they'd had to cut Livy and use suction to pull the child out. Livy saw the baby held high above her, glowing, red, wailing, a white rope still attaching them. She heard Christopher's ecstatic cry and the doctor's cheerful, "We've got a beautiful big baby girl!" She saw Christopher cutting the glowing white rope with the doctor's assistance. But she had not been able to join them in their festivities. Instead she began to shriek, "Let me die!" over and over again, and leaped off the table and fell to the floor screaming for them to just please kill her now, she could not take another second of this life. They'd finally had to calm her with a shot of Demerol.

When she woke up five hours later, Christopher was seated beside the bed holding the sleeping infant. He came to Livy smiling softly and said, "This is our girl." She'd been dreaming that she was involved in a local campaign to abolish vaginal births.

She had never known giving birth was so much like dying, or that, like dying, it went on so much longer than you expected it to. And that afterward you were not the same. She'd been in therapy for half a decade at that point, turning the details of her difficult childhood over and over, but after the birth she quit. The child she'd been, she felt, was dead now, and therefore not worth discussing.

Livy's mother was her first visitor at the hospital. She walked in bearing a cup of Starbucks chai, Livy's favorite comfort drink—but somehow the sight of it made Livy sad. "You poor thing," her mother said, and from the way she looked at her, Livy knew that her mother knew she had died on the birthing table. The girl she had been was no longer.

Her mother stayed with them for days after the birth, the same mother who had in part been responsible for the problems of Livy's childhood, the same mother who had been the subject of so many blistering therapy sessions. And yet as Livy sat there trying to nurse the baby, all she could feel toward her mother was warmth and sadness—and awe too, that she had come through the science fiction of birth four times and somehow gone on with the pedestrian task of raising her children. In those early days Livy sat for hours watching Dessa's tiny face and thinking, sometimes whispering aloud, "I'm sorry, I'm sorry"—for what, she couldn't say, only that she'd felt the need to apologize.

———— • ◆ • ————

Ramona leaned forward. "So listen, I have to tell you a secret." She glanced in at Christopher. "I'm switching careers."

"To what?"

Ramona paused, studied Livy's face for a moment, then said, "Don't laugh, but I'm studying to become a life coach."

Livy laughed a little. "What do you mean?"

"There's this institute in Union Square. I go for six weeks and get an accreditation—something to put on my wall. But the fact is, I'm already qualified. I already have my first client."

"You're not going to practice law anymore?"

"Oh, I'll still do it, sure, select clients, but this is where I want to put the bulk of my energy." Ramona paused, squinted out at the mountains. "My client, Lizette, is just the tip of the iceberg. Do you realize how many rich women there are, our age and older, desperately in need of coaching? I mean, powerful women, but they're overweight and lonely. I have this idea: I can combine life coaching with being a personal trainer. See, with Lizette, she's the head of a corporation, and her time is limited, so I coach her on her life while we work on her body at the gym. At first we did it together to save time, but I realized and she realized that it actually works better that way. The mind-body connection, you know. Adrenaline. Everything about it just works. So I thought—why not make it my signature? Nobody else is doing life coaching this way."

Ramona spoke fast, her eyes trained on Livy's face. She rolled her wineglass between her hands as if it were a magic lantern. A copy of *O Magazine* Ramona had brought off the plane sat on the small wrought-iron table between them, Oprah's maniacally happy face bursting off yet another issue.

Ramona's cell phone sat beside the magazine, a small silver thing the shape of a suppository. She'd made a show of turning off the sound when they settled out on the patio with their wine, but every few minutes Livy could see the phone light up and Ramona would pick it up and glance at the screen, and although she put it down each time, Livy had the sense she was itching to talk to whoever had called.

From inside the house she could hear Christopher whistling as he cooked, the sizzle of something hitting the pan. She felt a wave of longing for Ramona to be gone, longing to be alone with Christopher and Dessa again. She had the sense of being intruded upon, as if something not exactly dangerous, but certainly foreign, had entered their home.

"He seems awfully sweet, Livy," Ramona said, narrowing her eyes as she stared in at Christopher through the glass. "It must be nice to be taken care of."

"Well, I still work," Livy said, but she let the sentence trail off because she worked less, so much less, than she had when they'd both lived in New York.

Ramona was still watching Christopher, but some dark memory flickered across her sharp features.

Livy couldn't help but ask. "Do you ever think about Julian these days? Do you miss him?"

Ramona shrugged. "Not much. I hear things. He's living with a rich white guy now in Chelsea. Can you believe it? Some trust fund brat. They attend a Unitarian church and are interviewing surrogates. Julian found God and wants to have a baby.

He goes around telling all our old friends how once he was lost but now he's found. He's never been happier in his life. I was his period of self-hatred. That's what I represent to him." She shook her head, smirking. "These mixed dudes, you gotta watch out. They start out one thing and end up another. I mean, does anybody know who Julian really is?"

They were both quiet then, letting the words about Julian hang there over them.

Livy remembered going to sit with Ramona in those weeks after her assault, after Julian moved out. The house was airless, stuffy with grief, and Ramona sat on the couch under an afghan with the television flickering nonsense before her, alternating between sleep and deep, frightening, guttural sobs that seemed they might break a blood vessel. Livy kept repeating, "You're going to be all right, you're going to get through this," but really she had not been so sure.

— ◆ —

At Ramona's request, Livy had booked them a day at the spa. It was world famous, a faux-Buddhist retreat about twenty miles out of town. Livy had heard of the place but had never been.

She had printed out a description of the spa from the Internet and Ramona read from it in the car. They'd picked the Buddha Day Special. "Oh, this sounds delicious," Ramona said. "We get an hour in a private hot tub, a deep tissue massage, something called a salt glow scrub, and a craniosacral massage. And some free soap." She clucked her tongue. "It's criminal that you live so close and have never been to this place. I'd be here all the time if I were you."

"It's hard when you have a baby," Liv said, "hard to get away for hours on end."

"Livy, girl, this is something I've been meaning to say to you," Ramona said. "You've got to start pampering yourself. Just because you're a mom doesn't mean that has to stop. You need to take little day trips with friends. A massage. A well-rested mother is a relaxed mother is a good mother—"

But they had arrived. At the end of the gravel parking lot, a line of Japanese lanterns led up a long stairwell to the entrance, and beyond was a stone room with a fountain gurgling in the center.

———⋄———

In the changing room Livy saw that Ramona had brought a bathing suit—a bright fuchsia bikini to wear during the Jacuzzi part of their package.

"Oh God, a bathing suit, I forgot to bring one," Livy said, embarrassed. She had not even read the description of what they would be doing. "Should I just wear underwear?"

Ramona shrugged. "Whatever makes you comfortable, Liv. Plenty of women go naked. You should go in your birthday suit. No shame in your game." Her eyes flickered over Livy where she stood in her plain black cotton bikini bottom, worn thin from repeat washings, and a nursing bra that flapped open to reveal her nipples. "Girl, we need to take you lingerie shopping." Ramona wore a delicate cream-colored lace thong and a matching push-up bra, the bikini laid out before her on a bench. She examined herself in the mirror as she spoke. "Not for the guys or anything. It's to make you feel good about yourself."

"I already feel good," Livy said, but as she spoke she caught a glimpse of her body next to Ramona's. She looked like a mom—the kind of woman she had sworn she would never become when she was living in New York.

She followed Ramona up a stone path to the private outdoor bath area, feeling impatient. She was eager for the three hours of spa bliss to be over. She wouldn't admit it to Ramona, but she missed Dessa—the weight and smell of her body, her bewildered black eyes—and she missed Christopher. She missed the three of them, they were a unit now. She would miss the quiet evening ritual—bathing the baby, feeding the baby, showing the baby her video before rocking her to sleep. Once they put her down in the nursery with the white noise machine beside her crib, Christopher would start cooking while Livy played sous chef or cleaned up the mess of the day and music played from the radio or the television droned in the background. They relished those adult evenings of wine and food and talk—not because Dessa was absent but because she was present, her sleep the grand prize in the other room. After dinner they would read in bed, side by side, the smell of lavender floating in from the desert darkness outside, or listen to jazz, or make love, or take a bath together, or watch something trashy on television.

They were in the bubbling Jacuzzi now, under a canopy of trees. Livy was naked and Ramona, in her bikini, was telling her a story about her latest man mishap. She'd been seeing another lawyer, somebody she met at her neighborhood Starbucks. He was a white guy, Jewish, stout—cute, but nothing like the golden peacock Julian had been. Ramona said she felt safe with him. A few weeks into them sleeping together, she walked past his computer and saw he had ads open from "JDate," the Jewish matchmaking service. She asked him about it and he said, matter-of-factly, that he found her ravishing, but that he planned to marry a Jewish woman someday.

"I was his thirty minutes of difference," Ramona said. "I'm swearing off white boys and mixed nuts. Mark my words: I'm going black and I'm never going back."

They both laughed together the way they used to do, only Julian had been with them laughing too back then, like a third girlfriend.

They sat quietly then, waiting for the front desk to call them to their next treatment. The only sound was the gurgling from the jet under the water.

"So, Livy, tell me," Ramona said into the darkness. "Are you and Christopher happy?"

She couldn't see Ramona's expression, but her voice sounded hungry. Livy recalled all the evenings she'd spent in her old life, bonding with her other single women friends. It was like some ancient ritual, the way they offered each other their tales of love lives gone wrong, men behaving badly, how they offered up their dissatisfaction and ambivalence like pieces of fruit at the feet of the Buddha.

"I'm happy, yes," Livy said, and it was mostly true. And yet even as she said it, she felt a longing for her old self, poor little Livy Thurman, the old maid of Brooklyn. That lonely misery of hers had made her, in a sense, one with other women. That misery of hers had made her feel that her life had not only a plot but also an audience. It wasn't that she didn't have problems anymore, but they were of a different tenor—both quieter and graver. And they remained private: It was Christopher she would talk to about them, not the girlfriends.

She heard distant thunder now, and hoped it would rain while they were in the hot tub. But it sounded too far away.

She recalled a summer when she was a kid and her family had rented a vacation house on an island off Cape Cod. A week into their stay, there was a hurricane warning. The whole island went into a state of hysteria. Her mother and father made emergency preparations: taped the windows, filled the tub with water, stocked the pantry with canned goods and batteries. Livy remembered how much she'd loved the feeling of being safely locked inside with all of them, her brothers and sister and mother and father. The hurricane never materialized, but she'd enjoyed the threat of it so much it didn't matter.

Marriage had given her a similar feeling—that she was, with Christopher, battening down the hatches against the hurricane.

There were so many lonely souls getting knocked around in the storm out there, the way she had been, but now she was inside, with Christopher and Dessa, huddled together for warmth.

The rest of the spa date felt interminable to her, the endless ablutions. A little hippie woman massaged her and salted her and basted her with ointments. Livy kept an eye on the clock through it all, imagining Dessa's bedtime ritual going on without her, imagining Christopher sitting down to dinner without her.

When at last it was over she wasted no time showering and dressing, but Ramona took her time. She groaned and stretched and rubbed her belly. "Do you realize I still haven't gone? Jesus. I'm not going to eat another bite, I swear, until I've gotten this out of me," she said, brushing her hair in front of the mirror. After that she did deep breathing exercises and massaged her temples, and examined her toned and glowing figure in the mirror. She slathered herself with yet more oils and serums. She put on her expensive lingerie and stood beside Livy, who was already dressed in her jeans and T-shirt. Ramona stared at them both in the mirror as she spoke.

"That was amazing, girl, wasn't it amazing?" She put an arm around Livy's shoulder and squeezed. "Now promise me you'll do stuff like this more often. Promise me that you'll come back and really start taking care of yourself."

Livy nodded and said, "I promise," though she knew she would never come back.

Ramona squeezed her shoulder again and stared into her own eyes as she said, "If I've accomplished anything on this visit, it's to make you take better care of yourself."

Livy saw herself beside her friend—small, ten pounds overweight, with stretch marks and that belly and those rings of exhaustion under her eyes. She looked older. And Ramona looked strangely victorious to her. It was as if once again Livy had performed a public service. Ramona had come to New Mexico to see poor Livy Thurman's dowdy life as a wife and mother, to discover that Livy's husband wore clogs and her baby was fat and demanding, and that Livy herself wore raggedy old cotton underwear and had given up on herself. It was as if Ramona had come to New Mexico to see just how awful married life, mother-life, could be—and she would leave newly reassured of the superiority of her life being single, free, back in the city.

• ◆ •

Christopher was asleep in bed with his reading glasses on and a book open on his chest.

Ramona and Livy tiptoed around the kitchen, fixing themselves glasses of water.

Before they said good night, Ramona checked her cell phone and, smiling, whispered, "This guy I met at the gym keeps texting me," then disappeared into the guest bedroom, her eyes still on the phone.

———•◆•———

Livy remembered most clearly the evening she got back from her first meeting with Christopher in Santa Fe. On the cab ride from JFK to Brooklyn, she'd stared out at the gray dusky light over the city, thinking that after New Mexico it looked like a trash heap to her. She had just landed in a heap of trash.

Back in her apartment, she'd unpacked her new cowboy hat and propped it on a shelf. She took a shower and put on her new turquoise nightgown.

It was over. She knew, sitting on the slim modern sofa in her Brooklyn walk-up, that it was over, this romance with herself. A love affair was ending. And she felt a new affection for her solitary life, the same affection that sometimes arises for the person you are about to leave.

———•◆•———

She woke in the dark, to the sound of Dessa crying. The clock read 5:22.

She opened the door to the nursery to find Dessa standing in her crib, her face crumpled and red, screaming.

She picked Dessa up and Dessa stopped crying and hugged Livy around her neck.

"There, now, baby, Mama's here. Mama's here."

It still amazed her how quickly the child's mood could shift. She smiled and cooed on the changing table as Livy took off her wet diaper and put on a new one. The sky outside the window was changing too—it had gone from black to a heartbreaking pink in the time it took to put Dessa's pajamas back on. She picked up the child and opened the door to the nursery. Ramona was standing there, holding her empty water glass.

"Oh God, you scared me," Livy said with a laugh.

Ramona looked different. She was still wearing the cream-colored thong and a tank top, but she wore a silk bandanna around her head, and without her makeup Livy could see she still had a scar from the attack so many years ago, a faint, jagged line beneath her hairline.

"Guess what?" Ramona said, smiling.

"What?"

"I went."

"You went?"

"Yep," Ramona said. She followed Livy into the kitchen, where she refilled her glass. "I don't know, maybe it was the massage, or maybe it was all the stuff the naturopath gave me the other day, but, girl, I'm completely empty."

She leaned on the counter as if she was getting ready to talk.

"That's great," Livy said, shifting Dessa in her arms.

Dessa had been quiet, but now she began to whimper and pull at Livy's nightgown.

"I have to go nurse her," Livy said.

"Oh," Ramona said. "Sure. I'm going to go out for a jog. I feel so light."

Livy headed downstairs, where the curtains still shrouded

the room in darkness. She slid into bed beside Christopher, placing the child between them. It was their usual ritual. She pulled down her nightgown and Dessa lay on her side and filled herself with Livy's milk.

Christopher, half asleep, reached across the child to touch Livy's hair. "Everything okay?"

"Ramona finally went," she whispered.

"Went where?"

"To the bathroom. She finally took a dump."

"Wonderful," he said, and she couldn't tell if he was joking or sleep-talking, because in the next instant he was breathing heavily, asleep again beside her.

———— ·◆· ————

Mothers know this: Babies come into this world with their souls already forged.

Christopher had taken a picture of Dessa in those first moments after she'd been ripped from Livy, when she was just a nameless wet thing. In the photo she looks glistening and enormous, clean and somehow indignant, always and already the child she would become.

And sooner or later, all women know this: There is no way to do it right. You cannot have it all. Something has to give. You won't know what it was you gave up until it is too late to recover.

———— ·◆· ————

The delivery hurt plenty, but nobody had warned Livy about the pain during the days following the birth, after the adrenaline had worn off. That was when the real suffering began.

Movies never show this part, the days in the hospital when you feel as if a Mack truck has driven out of you and left you a gaping bloody hole, and the thought of taking a bowel movement is so terrifying that when it finally happens you sit on the toilet weeping and it is there that you find religion, on the toilet, it is there you find yourself asking God to spare you this pain, but God doesn't come to save you, only the shit comes and it is as bad as you have imagined, worse somehow than the baby, a reenactment of the terrible crime, but this time with no drugs to thwart it and no Lamaze breathing to distract you and no partner holding your hand and no baby's glistening face to justify it, just the cold hospital bathroom, the squeegie bottle full of cold water, the tearing hard bowel movement opening the dirty stitches, and the hospital-grade perpetually soaked maxipad, fit for a female giant.

The nurse who checked her down there that night stared aghast at the situation between Livy's legs. "That baby really tore you up."

In the weeks after the birth, the world turned inside out. Black became white. Day became night and night became day. Lovers became fathers. And Livy found aging mothers—the heavyset women with the weathered faces and the weary eyes, their soft bulging bellies like ghosts of long-gone pregnancies—to be the most beautiful creatures on the planet. The young, childless women, with their taut skin and flat stomachs and anticipatory smiles, were not ugly to her, just meaningless, their beauty like grape juice to wine. She fell in love with mothers everywhere. How had they done it? Livy was bewildered, humbled in the face of the question. She felt slain by childbirth. For a moment, at least, it equalized everything. White women, black women, yellow women, brown women, poor women, rich women—mothers, all of them. They met in waiting rooms and buses and toy stores and playgroups and one of them always asked the first question—How old is the baby?—and then took it from there. They talked about milestones and nursing difficulties and those last ten pounds they couldn't lose and peanut allergies and diaper rashes, and yet beneath the pedestrian chatter Livy felt overtaken with love of a religious magnitude for all of them. She felt the daughter-self, young and vain, dying, and the mother-self, huge and sad, rising up in its wake, linking her to nothing less than history.

Until you are a mother you are blameless. *Now you are on the other side of history*, Livy thought, staring around at the weary faces of the other mothers. *Now you are dirty.*

———— • ◆ • ————

In the sunlight, beside her in the Jeep on the way back to the Old Hotel, Livy saw Ramona as she had always seen her, as perhaps she had always been since she came, wet and screaming, into this world. Her spirit was like a hummingbird, an always-moving, half-here, half-gone thing. Even now, she was two places at once: here, with Livy in a Jeep in Santa Fe, and at the same time back in her life in New York, with her life-coaching clients and her love interests.

She was talking about Lizette, her client, who had called her the night before, crying, saying she'd broken her diet and was on the verge of quitting her six-figure job. "That woman is a hot mess. She needs me. The work just feels so exciting. I'm really making a difference in her life."

The airport shuttle van was already there when they pulled into the hotel parking lot. Livy helped Ramona with her bags.

Ramona chattered on, upbeat. "I had a fabulous time, girl. You're doing so well with all the changes. You promise me you're going to take better care of yourself? Use that spa. Buy some nice lingerie. Splurge."

"Okay." Livy said, no longer offended by the advice. "I'll do that."

"We should do this again. Maybe every two years we should meet in a different place."

"That sounds great," Livy said.

"Next time let's go to Costa Rica. I have this client who owns a resort there—" Midsentence, Ramona went quiet, squinting into the distance at the mountains. When she looked at Livy her face was a bare frightened thing.

"Was I just blind? How did I miss it?"

It took Livy a beat. Julian. They had returned to Julian.

"Nobody saw it coming," she said. "He had issues. They had nothing to do with you."

"Seven years," Ramona said. She bit her lip, her eyes welling up. "Can you imagine?"

"Hey," Livy said, taking Ramona in her arms, patting her back. Ramona smelled like the city itself, something floral and hard, and yet she felt frail and limp as a child in Livy's arms.

"Don't be afraid," Livy whispered. "Be brave. You have to be brave." As she said it, she imagined once more the old self, the one who sat in the leather chair, facing Ramona and Julian, the couple on the couch. She missed the old Livy like a lost sister, missed and loved the brave little sister, saw her in the dark Brooklyn night, walking toward her ice-coated car, head turned down against the cold.

When Ramona pulled away, she was smiling. "Hey, did I tell you I have a date tomorrow night? The one from the gym. He's kind of young, but fine —" She stopped, let out a short laugh, and then she was walking away through the bright maze of cars, turning back to blow a kiss before she climbed inside the van.

· You Are Free ·

The writer had misspelled her name on the envelope the way people usually did—as "Laura" rather than "Lara" (her mother's idea of exotic). Inside, the letter itself was written on ruled paper torn from a spiral-bound notebook, the curly edges making a kind of fringe. The letter began:

Dear Ms. Barrows,

Please don't throw this letter out until you have read it and heard my side of the story. I was put up for adoption in 1983 when I was two days old. Ever since I turned eighteen, I have been looking to find my birth mother. Recently, a change in the law has allowed me to see the records. This new information has led me to the definite conclusion that you are the person I've been searching for. I was real happy to

*see that you lived so close by. Don't worry. I'm not angry and
I'm not blaming you for what happened. I'm sure you have
your reasons. I don't know if you want to meet me after all
these years. I understand if you don't. I really do. But please
write me back.*

Sincerely,
Mandy L. Doheny

Under her name was an address in Paterson, New Jersey,
and a phone number.

Lara tossed the letter on top of her other mail—a DMV notice and a *Star* magazine—and began to make herself dinner,
a packet of ramen noodles with shrimp flavoring. She considered whether to write the woman back and tell her she'd made
a mistake. She sat down to eat her noodles in front of the TV.

Later, she ran a bath and lay in it in the dark, trying to relax.
She'd read once that people who took baths lived longer than
people who took showers, so she took a bath every night. After
she dried off, she slathered on lotion, then put on sweatpants
and a T-shirt and went to watch the news. The letter still lay
there on the coffee table. She picked it up and stared at it.

She wondered how the woman had gotten her name, and
how she'd found her address. Lara had an unlisted number. She
had just had her first byline, but it was in an obscure magazine called *The Charitable America*, which had published only
one issue so far. The magazine was the brainchild of a young

man named Timothy Fitzgerald, known to all as "Fitz," who had gone to journalism school with Lara. *The Charitable American* was geared toward the top one percent income bracket, whom it was supposed to inspire and educate on giving their money away. Fitz had called Lara and invited her to be on staff. Her official title was contributor, which meant she got no health insurance or retirement plan. She was essentially freelance, which was just as well since she didn't expect Fitz's magazine to last. It was just another niche magazine, like *Plumpers* or *Vacation Yachts*; it wasn't even sold on newsstands, but was given away for free in doctors' offices and at promotional events. She figured it would last a few issues and get some press until Timothy's stepfather, who was funding the entire venture, realized nobody really wanted to read about giving money away and pulled the plug. In the meantime, Lara would pick up a few monthly paychecks.

That night Lara tossed the letter from Mandy L. Doheny in the trash, on top of the remains of her ramen noodles with shrimp flavoring. Then she closed the lid and went to bed.

———— ◆ ————

She sat in her cubicle in the corner of the fifth floor of a building in midtown Manhattan, trying to finish the story she'd been working on for weeks.

An eighty-five-year-old black woman from Tennessee named Iola Brooks, who had worked her whole life as a washerwoman, had saved every penny she earned in a secret bank account.

Recently, with no children of her own and no husband, Iola Brooks had decided to give the entire amount—$150,000—to the local university. The media had gone wild for the story. The Republican state senator and the university president were milking the publicity for all it was worth, and had been flying the old woman around the country to appear on talk shows and to be interviewed by newspapers and magazines and on the radio.

Iola Brooks would grace the cover of the next issue of *The Charitable American*. Lara would get her first cover byline.

Lara had interviewed Iola Brooks a few weeks earlier in the lobby of the Waldorf-Astoria. Neat as a pin, with straightened white hair pulled back in a tight bun, she'd answered Lara's questions in a meek, soft southern drawl.

"Is there anything you still want to do with your life?" Lara had asked before they parted ways.

Iola looked out the window of the bar at the stream of business suits marching past. She seemed wistful. "I want to go to San Francisco," she said, "and see that golden bridge. I sure would love to see a golden bridge."

Lara had not had the heart to tell the old lady that the bridge was not really made of gold.

———— • ◆ • ————

She finished the story at the eleventh hour and went out for a drink with her friend Jose.

Lara was thirty-three years old—the same age as Jesus when

he was hung up to die. She was thirty-three, the same numbers that showed on her clock radio when she woke at 3:33 each morning with what she called "the rattles." She'd been getting the rattles for as long as she could remember. She would wake up to find the bed shaking ever so slightly. It wasn't a ghost and it wasn't an earthquake. It was the vibration of her own heart, which at that hour felt strong enough to shake the foundation of the bed.

"You finish the story on that old black lady?" Jose asked, scanning the bar over her head for fresh meat.

"Iola Brooks?"

"Yeah, the old coot who gave all her money away. Why'd she give her money to a bunch of good ol' boys who wouldn't even accept her as a student back in the day? Fool."

Lara sighed. "I don't know. Maybe she wants to be remembered. Maybe she wants to get into heaven."

"Whatever. Ignorance must be bliss," Jose said, his eyes still on the door behind her. "If I had a hundred thou? I'd go to Barneys and buy me that Prada coat. I'd buy an apartment in Tribeca and have it furnished by somebody with taste. I'd throw a big motherfucking party just because I could."

A handsome older man with expensive silver hair sidled up and slid his arm around Jose's waist, whispered something in his ear. Lara promised herself, for the umpteenth time, that she would not hang out with Jose in gay bars anymore.

"Can you excuse us for a moment?" Jose said. "I'm going to take this dance."

Lara took a cab home to Brooklyn, ignoring the driver's exasperated sigh when she told him he had to cross the bridge.

Tinker, her cat, mewed when she walked in the door. She flipped through the mail. Nothing. But when she pressed the button on her answering machine, a young woman. She didn't introduce herself by name, but she didn't have to. Lara knew that voice — it was as if she had always known that voice.

The woman had a working-class accent and spoke in a whisper, clear and insistent, but a whisper nonetheless. She sounded on the edge of tears, desperate and beseeching, so much so that, as Lara listened, she stepped away from the machine and crossed her arms and watched the black box, not breathing.

"I'm sorry to bother you again. I guess you got my letter. I been waiting to hear from you. I been hoping I can see you in person. I promise I won't mess up your life. I won't get in the way. I just want to know who you are. All my life I been wondering who was my mother and why didn't she want me. I just want to know why you gave me away. I'm sure you got your reasons. I don't blame you or nothin'. I just want to know. And then I will leave you alone and it'll be like nothing ever happened, if that's the way you want it to be." There was a pause, and Lara thought she could make out crying, the sound of a gasp, heavy breathing, then, "I don't want to be a pest. I just want us to meet. Please call me back. Okay?" She rattled off a phone number, then paused and said, "Oh yeah. I forgot to say. This is Mandy, your kid. Um, bye."

Lara stepped up to the machine and pressed Play again and

went to the couch and sat listening to the message all over again.

Mandy sounded young and she sounded rough, like somebody who had struggled.

Lara listened to the message a third time. This time she was prepared and jotted down the number.

She fingered the paper and listened to the neighbors fight, adult voices speaking harshly, the man in an unfamiliar language. Behind them, a child cried, a toddler. The kid didn't seem to be abused, exactly, but Lara had once seen him out on the porch at five in the morning, wearing diapers and a dirty T-shirt and wailing his heart out. It was a temperate day and he was safe enough, but they'd kept him out there for almost an hour, wandering in circles, clutching the rail, and staring down at the street. Lara knew because she fell back asleep and when she woke up an hour later he was still out there, sitting on the floor and rocking back and forth, his voice hoarse and his face crumpled. Lara called the police and waited by her window until they showed up. When they rang the doorbell, the father pulled the kid inside the apartment. Lara had tried to go back to sleep then, but she kept hearing the kid crying, as if he were still out on the porch.

She sat in the dark now, listening to the muffled misery next door. She'd seen the parents. They were unfriendly. The man was burly and foreign and unemployed. The wife was pale and thin, with bleached blond hair and a distracted, nervous air. The kid was cute enough, but wouldn't be for long.

She picked up the phone and dialed the number that Mandy L. Doheny had left for her.

A young woman answered on the second ring. "Hello?" she said. She sounded tired. Lara could hear a television in the background, the wild applause of a studio audience.

"Hello?" the woman said again. "Who's there?"

Lara could hear the television more clearly now. It sounded like a rerun of *Oprah*. Oprah's earthy, familiar voice was saying, "I want you to meet Gracie. She's got a story you won't believe."

"Hello?" the woman said once more, and then Lara could hear that she was turning down the volume on the television until it was silent. In a whisper, sounding as small and sad and desperate as she had on the answering machine, she said, "Is that you?"

Lara hung up.

The fighting next door was getting louder. Lara picked up the remote and turned on the TV to block it out. Oprah was wiping a tear away from her face while she held a young woman's hand, nodding her head and saying, "You're very brave."

Lara watched Oprah but didn't really see her. Her mind was filled with an image of Mandy sitting on a sofa in a dark apartment somewhere in New Jersey, watching this very same show, this very same exchange. Lara imagined not her face but her silhouette from behind, a young woman, thin and lost, framed by the light of a giant television set. She felt a tug of sadness, like loss or remorse. She wished she had said something to clarify the situation, like "I'm not your mother," but she had not been able to force the words out.

———◆———

In the middle of the night she woke to the bed shaking, the room shaking, her heart beating. The rattles. The fragments of a terrible dream cluttered her mind. A baby under a bed, crying. A dimly lit room, a table with stirrups, a smear of blood on a tiled wall. Her own voice as a child yelling, "Momma! Momma!"

The next morning Lara stood in her bedroom in front of the long mirror, staring at her naked body. She was thin, muscular, pale. She had small breasts, a swatch of dark curly hair between her legs. Everything about her body was tight and lean, and although she wasn't a virgin she had never had an orgasm. The last man with whom she'd had sex said she looked like a virgin, and indeed it hurt when he entered her the way it always hurt when a man pushed inside of her. Hers was not a body that had given birth to anything, ever.

And yet? She wondered. It was a crazy thought but it kept floating back to her, like some piece of rotten driftwood you can't swim away from. The summer of her thirteenth birthday was the same summer Mandy had been born and put up for adoption, a summer Lara remembered as dreary and lonely and hot. The summer her parents had had the kitchen renovated by Doug, a carpenter in his late twenties so blond and boyishly good-looking that all the mothers in the neighborhood wondered aloud why he wasn't taken. Once he entered the bathroom while Lara was taking a shower and pretended to wash his hands for an inordinately long time while he watched her reflection in the mirror. She didn't remember anything else about that moment, only lying in bed afterward, still wet and shivering, feeling shame. And then somehow she had gained weight and had gone into the hospital for what they'd told her was appendicitis. The doctors knocked her out and afterward she lay around the house eating Fudgsicles and watching a lot of *Three's Company*. She had not seen many friends and she had cried herself to sleep at night, but for what, she could not now remember.

———— • ◆ • ————

It was a rainy day and the subway smelled of wet bodies. There was a young woman across from her with a child in a stroller. The stroller was covered with plastic to keep out the rain or the germs or both. The child was maybe five, brown-skinned and wiry, with dreadlocks. He was sucking his thumb hard and staring listlessly out at the press of people beyond the plastic. His mother, alarmingly young, was talking to the girl beside her, saying in a thick, gruff voice that didn't match her own baby face, "That motherfucker tried to tell me it was just eczema. On his dick. I was like, *naw*."

Lara watched the girl's glossy lips move and thought that was the strange power of motherhood. No matter how badly, carelessly, halfheartedly, or unhappily one did it, you remained a mother. Bad mother, good mother, here mother, gone mother. The adjectives changed but the noun remained the same. You were a mother. There was no changing that.

———— • ◆ • ————

Iola Brooks had changed her mind.

The old black maid who had washed white people's clothes her whole life, only to give—poignantly, with a spirit of saintly forgiveness and goodwill—her entire life savings to the southern formerly segregated college, the old black lady who had traveled around the country, making appearances on *Oprah* and *Good Morning America* in her starched white church dress, her Bible held together with duct tape—that old black spinster with her meek "yes ma'am" and "no ma'am" and "I want to go to San Francisco and see that golden bridge," that same Iola Brooks had, at the last minute, before the final forms were signed and the money was handed over, rescinded her offer.

There was a message on Lara's machine when she got to work. It was from a weary-sounding university public relations officer, telling her to call the cover story off. Iola Brooks had decided to keep the money until she died, and when she died, what was left of her savings would go to her cousin Dionne and Dionne's three kids.

Lara called Iola Brooks to get the story from her directly. She answered on the third ring, and groaned, irritated, when Lara told her who she was.

"Lissen," she said, "I told those fools at the university I done changed my mind. Why won't they just leave me alone? They been calling me off the hook. Trying to convince me how this is gonna do something to change the world. I spent sixty-five years scrubbing the shit out their britches, why I owe them a cent?"

Lara let her ramble on. She knew the article would be cut. *The Charitable American* was meant to inspire people to give to the needy, and now any article on Iola Brooks would be about something else altogether.

Still, she had one more question.

What would Iola Brooks do with her remaining years on earth?

"Maybe I'll go on a cruise," Iola said. "Or maybe I'll buy me a new car and some pump jemsons." She went on to list all the things she might buy, now that she was not giving to charity. A Clapper. A set of Ginsu knives. A Chia Pet.

Finally Lara thanked her for her time and wished her the best of luck with her purchases.

"Finish the edits?" It was Fitz, leaning over her cubicle wearing a white smile and a polo shirt with the collar turned up.

"Kill the piece," Lara told him. "Iola Brooks has seen the error of her ways. She's decided to keep her money to herself after all."

She spent the rest of the afternoon in a story meeting, brainstorming with Fitz and his staff of dilettante friends about what might replace Iola Brooks on the cover. Fitz wouldn't look her in the eye and she got the feeling he was upset with her, as if she was somehow to blame for the old woman's change of heart. In the end, he assigned the new cover story—on the estate of Jerry Falwell—to somebody else.

At five o'clock she headed back to Brooklyn on the D train. It was only when she unlocked the door of her apartment and stepped inside and felt Tinker rub up against her ankle that she realized it had been with her all day, like a dull headache— the girl, that is, Mandy L. Doheny. She went to the answering machine, barely breathing. She saw that there had been two missed calls but there was no message. She didn't bother turning on the lights but sat in the dark with Tinker on her lap, stroking her soft fur. She tried to imagine what Mandy L. Doheny looked like, what she had looked like. She imagined a little girl—seven years old or so—small and dark and smiling as she ran toward her across a playground, a lunch box banging against her thigh. She imagined herself opening her arms wide to welcome the child into them.

She was crying now. Alone. She was crying alone in the dark. She felt the tears roll down her cheeks. They tickled, like crawling bugs, but she did not rub them away.

Lara had gotten an abortion her sophomore year in college. It was nothing shocking, nothing unusual. Everybody she knew had gotten one at some point, even more than one. She barely remembered the procedure. What was more vivid to her was the party she'd gone to a few nights later, the boy she'd refrained from having sex with only because she was still passing blood clots. That she remembered.

And she recalled her friend Karen, beautiful, tawny, strident Karen, who told her she was brave for going through with the procedure. A few months later, Karen had invited her to protest the local Domino's Pizza, because it had just come public that the owners were anti-abortion. After the protest they had gone and smoked a joint in Lara's dorm room, and after that they'd called Domino's and, laughing so hard they could barely get the words out, tried to order a pizza with fetus topping.

Lara was shivering now, cold, though she was still wearing her damp coat and the cat was hot and purring, its little heart beating, oblivious to the sobbing of the body beneath her.

A shrill sound. Ringing. The phone. Lara scrambled to her feet. Tinker, tossed to the floor, meowed in outrage.

She picked up the receiver. "Hello?" she said, gasping.

The voice that came back was like an echo, somebody else crying in the dark—a woman's voice, familiar as honey to her now.

"It's me. Why won't you see me? Don't you even care? Don't you even want to know what's happened to me?"

Lara said, "Okay. Yes. Okay."

She changed her outfit three times before she left the apartment that Sunday morning. Her heart beat with anticipation, even though she knew it was crazy. She had never had a baby. She would have remembered it. Lara was thirty-three and childless, manless, the case study of shrill magazine articles declaring the crisis of American women. She spent her Saturday nights with a cantankerous gay wit named Jose and sometimes his nebbishy sidekick, Lou. She ate her lunch with a copy editor named Francis, a person she knew on paper was a woman but in person thought of as an "it."

She was one of a million mid-thirties New Yorkers who had come to the city precisely to get free of family, free of suburbia, free of lawn gnomes and barbecue equipment, and whom now family life had passed by. It was getting late in the day for her to incorporate family into her life. She was a childless woman, and she suspected she would always be so. That was her fate, and she was trying hard to love her fate.

And yet. Here she was, all dressed up and going to meet a girl named Mandy L. Doheny, a girl who claimed to be her daughter.

She realized as she started out the door that the trepidation and doubt were not real. She had felt obligated to have those emotions. But they were false. She was elated. She felt giddy with the knowledge that she had a child out there. She had always thought of her life like a road, a straight road that stretched out ahead of her, beckoning her to the finish line, the grave. But now she knew she had always been a mother, and this fact made her life story look more like a circle than a road. She was moving forward and backward at the same moment. She had a family—a child—and the knowledge of this made her feel complete, though she knew she was not supposed to buy into such retrograde logic.

Mandy had suggested they meet at a Starbucks across from the Port Authority. She said she'd be sitting in the back of the café near the windows.

The subway was nearly empty except for a few early risers, immigrants with scrubbed faces and stiff outfits, on their way to church. Lara sat watching the underground darkness fly past out the window. She imagined the girl she was going to meet, imagined a young woman who looked just as she had looked at the age of twenty, a vague, almost fetal imprecision to her features, like somebody not yet fully born.

— ◆ —

A teenage boy stood behind the register wearing disposable gloves and placing small slices of pastry into paper sampling cups.

And in the back of the café, yes, a girl was seated by the windows. There was nobody else it could be. She sat beside a baby stroller, and was pushing it back and forth with one arm while she gazed out the window. And so this meant that Lara was not only a mother but a grandmother. She walked toward the girl, who was heavyset, with dirty blond hair pulled back in a tight ponytail. As Lara got closer, she saw that the girl had thin lips and thin eyebrows that had been plucked so many times they were almost gone. She didn't have any drink or food on the table in front of her.

When she looked up and saw Lara, a slight, hopeful smile crossed her lips.

"Are you the one?" she said, rising from her seat.

She was heavier from the waist down, with a bulge at her belly where a baby had recently been. Lara glanced into the stroller and saw an infant, only a few months old, snuggled in blankets, asleep. The girl wore a white Adidas tracksuit and a thick gold chain around her neck with a nameplate that spelled out MANDY in bubbly cursive.

Lara stepped forward, held out her hand, trying to sustain her belief. But it was inescapably clear to her that there had been a mistake. This girl was no more her daughter than the pimply kid working the register. And she knew too that it was indeed her appendix she'd had removed in the summer of 1983. She didn't remember the summer or the surgery clearly, but that was what they'd removed, not a child, never a child.

She had to get it over with quickly so the girl would stop smiling at her like that. "Yes, I'm Lara, but there's been a mistake. I'm not your mother."

Mandy pulled her hand away, wiped it on her jeans, looked out the window, expressionless. "Why'd you come here, then?"

Lara looked down at the table. There were pieces of shredded napkin scattered all over it. "I thought there might be a chance."

"How do you know it's not true?" Mandy said, facing Lara now, but her eyes focused just slightly to the left of Lara's face.

"I just know."

The girl wanted to be sure. She showed Lara her documents, rumpled official forms, a nameless birth certificate from 1983, and a more recent letter from a Catholic charity that revealed the identity of her real mother, someone named Laura Barrows from Queens, who had been twenty-six at the time of Mandy's birth, not thirteen.

Mandy didn't cry when Lara pointed out the discrepancy. She just pursed her lips and nodded her head and said, "I get it, you ain't my mother," like somebody who was more accustomed to disappointment than to pleasant surprises.

Lara, just to be polite, asked the girl a few questions, and learned that she lived with her boyfriend, Jervey, in Paterson, New Jersey. The baby in the stroller, who was still asleep, was named Jermajesty. He was Jervey's kid. She had another child too, from an earlier relationship, a three-year-old girl named Destiny. She learned that Mandy worked in a Subway sandwich shop. She learned that Mandy had been raised in foster care.

Mandy asked if Lara would watch the baby while she went to the bathroom. Lara nodded and Mandy excused herself and was gone. Almost as soon as the heavy metal door had closed, Jermajesty woke up, screaming. He was a tiny baby but he could make a lot of noise. Lara looked around but the boy at the register didn't seem to notice and she saw he had earphones in his ears as he cleaned an espresso machine with a white cloth. Lara

pushed the stroller back and forth, hoping the motion would
calm the baby, but he kept screaming. She'd forgotten how
much she disliked being around babies. It was their weight and
their ferociousness, rather than their smallness and vulnerabil-
ity, that scared her. They were strong and they were tenacious.

She looked toward the bathroom door, willing Mandy to
come out, but after a few minutes, when the door remained
closed, Lara picked the baby up and held him against her
shoulder as a friend with a baby had forced her to do every time
she visited, until gradually she'd stopped visiting at all. "There,
there," she said, hearing the strangeness of those familiar sooth-
ing words. "There, there." After a moment, Jermajesty began to
calm down, and then he stopped crying entirely. She was afraid
to stop moving, so she kept walking back and forth, patting the
baby's back.

As she paced, she thought about Iola Brooks, and how Iola
wanted to visit "that golden bridge" before she died. Lara had
gone to college in San Francisco, not far from that bridge. It was
in that very landscape she'd gotten pregnant and in that place
she'd undone what was growing inside of her. She had only a
moment's doubt the night before the procedure, when she'd
woken, suffused in a state of premature grief. She'd smothered
her sobs into her pillow for fear of waking her roommate, but was
dry-eyed and enthusiastic when Karen came beeping outside the
dormitory in the morning in her dented Volvo sports coupe.

The bridge they crossed that day was not golden. It was made
of steel and painted orange. They drove over it on the way back

from the procedure. Karen chattered about a psychology exam and a boy named Cricket. Lara, bleary and cramping beside her, looked out at the water and the cliffs in the distance, repeating a mantra, words aimed at somebody who didn't exist: *You are free, you are free, you are free.*

—◦—◆—◦—

The door opened and Mandy stepped out. Her eyes looked puffy and red, like maybe she'd been crying.

"I gotta get back," she said. "Jervey's no good with the other one."

Roughly, she took Jermajesty from Lara's arms and put him back in his stroller, covering him with blankets though it was warm inside the café. He started to cry again but she put a bottle of formula in his mouth and he went quiet.

"Took me two hours to get here on the bus," Mandy said, eyeing the pastries behind the glass. "Wasted the whole morning on this."

She was trying to make Lara feel guilty and it was working.

"Can I get you anything? For your bus ride home?"

"A Frappuccino, I guess."

Lara nodded. "Sure." They went to the register and Lara ordered the girl a Frappuccino. As she pulled out her wallet to pay, Mandy asked if she could get a piece of coffee cake with it, and an orange juice. Lara added the coffee cake and the orange juice to the order.

"And a vanilla milk for Jermajesty? In case he gets hungry?"

The baby looked too young to drink Starbucks vanilla milk—
it was probably for Destiny, the toddler at home—but Lara
agreed to it anyway.

They left Starbucks together and stood on the sidewalk. The
baby, still sucking his bottle, squinted out from beneath the
mound of blankets, a little elfin yellow face that made Lara's
heart hurt to look at.

Mandy wrapped her coffee cake in some napkins and put it,
with the other items, into her purse. It was still early for a Sunday, a gray autumn morning, and Broadway was as empty as
Lara had ever seen it.

"Good luck with your search for your mother," Lara said,
holding out her hand. "I hope you find her."

Mandy took Lara's hand and clasped it weakly. "Thanks for
the Frappuccino and stuff." She shrugged. "I hope you find
your kid, the one you gave away."

Lara started to clarify, but Mandy was already moving away,
across the wide intersection with her stroller. Lara waited until
they were safely inside the bus terminal before she looked away.

· Triptych ·

1. CHERRIES IN WINTER

Andrea smells what's happening under the table, but she doesn't say anything. It doesn't seem appropriate to mention, given the circumstances. Nobody else says a word either. They just eat their food in silence. A new one floats up, and Andrea tries to hold her breath as she takes another bite of turkey. It's more difficult than she imagined, to eat without breathing.

Andrea's mother died yesterday. She died quietly, all drugged up, in a white room surrounded by black nurses. It was a planned death, like a planned pregnancy. Everybody had plenty of time to mourn before the official end. Relatives from both sides have come to town for the funeral, which will be held tomorrow, and the aura at the table now is one of suppressed relief, and impatience for the ceremony to be over.

The last time Andrea saw her mother was two weeks ago, in the hospice in New Haven. Her breasts were gone and she wore a bandanna on her head, so that she looked like a young boy. So pale, she looked almost see-through. She drifted in and out of awareness, but when she was awake, all she could talk about was cherries: the blood red of them, the sweetness of them, the coolness of them, the pebblelike roundness of the pit rolling over her tongue. Andrea went all around New Haven that cold gray day looking for cherries, but they were out of season, and when she came back to the hospice her mother was not talking about cherries anymore. Her eyes were closed and it was time for Andrea to catch the train back to campus.

A new smell wafts up from under the table. It's unbelievable that such a small dog could make such a big impact on the world. Andrea holds a napkin over her mouth and eyes the other guests. They scrape at their plates unhappily.

"Pass the gravy, Andrea," her father says, nodding his big head toward the bowl. He looks fatter than he did two weeks ago. The weight sits on his chest, where it's supposed to be most deadly. She hands him the gravy.

Aunt Mabel made all the food. She and Uncle Gus drove from Syracuse this morning with a whole trunkload of steamy Tupperware.

"Have you chosen a major?" Gus asks her from across the table.

"Fine arts."

"Better than crude arts." He snorts with laughter.

Andrea just nods and takes another sip of wine.

Through the window above Gus's head, she can see it has

begun to snow. Soft flakes drift down and make a home on the branches of the apple tree where she used to sit, hiding from the world. She went there for many reasons, but the one she remembers most is her father. Once, it was her runny nose that made him angry. He couldn't stand the sight of it. He saw it as evidence of stupidity. He came after her holding a car key wrapped in toilet paper. He wanted to pick her nose, but he didn't want to use his finger, so he'd made this prosthesis. Andrea shrieked and sobbed and squirmed out of his grip, and made it up the apple tree before he could catch her.

In adulthood, her runny nose had turned into chronic nasal congestion and sinusitis. A wan vegetarian in her dorm suggested she might be allergic to wheat and dairy. Last month she stopped eating either, and her nose is now a clear and easy passageway. She thinks that if her nose were still blocked she wouldn't be able to smell the stench coming from under the table. Another fart floats up just then, a real doozy. Aunt Mabel coughs into her napkin.

"Jesus fucking Christ," her father says, rising. His chair falls to the floor behind him. "Where is that damn dog?"

He reaches under the table and she hears a yelp as Atticus is dragged from his hiding place. Atticus is old, nearly toothless. He was her mother's dog, a replacement baby for when Andrea got too old to hold, and she used to take him everywhere. Now he sleeps almost all the time. Her father grips the dog by the scruff of his neck and belts him once, twice across the rump. The dog scurries away whimpering, his tail between his legs.

Her father picks up his fallen chair, looks down at the table, daring anybody to say a word.

Uncle Gus snorts with laughter. "I thought it was you all that time, Bob."

Aunt Mabel laughs a little and everybody goes back to their food.

Except Andrea. She stares out the window, where the snow is falling harder. When she was a kid, Andrea used to play a game at dinner: She would imagine that she was a passerby on the street out front, somebody who just happened to glance in through their picture window at this dinner scene. She would imagine herself and her family through that stranger's eyes: a red-faced and bearded fat man at the head of the table, a slightly haggard woman serving food from the kitchen, a pudgy girl with braces feeding scraps to the dog under the table. Would they see this scene and think, *Happy Family? The American Dream?* Or would they notice the details: the swiftness with which the father belted back his glasses of scotch. How his voice grew louder and more slurred with each course. Would they know just from looking that some nights after dinner, his rage ended with that small woman bloody and bruised and weeping? On those nights, Andrea would lie in the dark, holding her pillow and praying to some faceless Sunday school God that her mother not die yet. She never guessed her mother's death would come from the inside out—a passing of the most pedestrian and blameless variety.

Triptych

———◆———

Andrea lies in the dark of her bedroom staring at the embers of her teenaged self. A poster of Harrison Ford still hangs above her bed, another of Jennifer Beals from *Flashdance* beside her dresser mirror. Her stomach makes unhappy sounds. Aunt Mabel's turkey isn't sitting well with her, but somehow she drifts off to sleep.

She wakes sometime later in the darkness to the sound of beeping garbage trucks outside.

Her mother looked almost beautiful in that hospice bed, androgynous and tiny, translucent. The last thing she said to Andrea: "What I wouldn't do for a nice cold bowl of cherries."

Andrea gets up and goes to the bathroom off the hall with the puffy pink toilet seat that makes a sighing noise when she sits down on it. It's only 4:30 a.m. She heads back to her room but instead of getting back into bed she dresses in the dark, then goes outside and sits in her father's Chevy with the motor running, letting it warm up before she rolls slowly out of the driveway.

Connecticut is an embalmed state. The houses sit like taxidermy, their marble eyes watching her as she cruises past. The Star Market is open, although the parking lot is empty. She doesn't know if it's been open all night or has just now opened for the morning. A man stands behind a table, under a sign that says ENSURE: COMPLETE, BALANCED NUTRITION FOR A HEALTHIER YOU. Behind him is a sculpture of bottles with the same words on them. When she moves past, he holds up a Dixie cup with white fluid in it. It reminds her of the hospital, the fluids that flowed in and out of her mother. "Would you like to try Ensure?" She shakes her head and moves on toward the produce department.

The fruit is piled neatly, identical apples and identical pears, not a mark on their waxy skins. There are cherries too, imported from Peru, at $5.99 a pound. She fills a bag until it can't hold any more.

Outside, the sky has begun to brighten. She sits in the Chevy with the motor running, eating the cherries. They don't taste very sweet. They are dry, rubbery things, and after a few tries, she sets them on the seat next to her.

She remembers that afternoon so many years ago, when her mother came home to find Andrea perched in the tree, still hiding from her father. Her mother put her hands on her hips and laughed at the sight. "Is that a monkey up there?" she called up. "Come on down, sweetie pie, I need your help."

That evening, Andrea sat at the kitchen table and snapped green beans and watched her mother move around, cooking dinner and humming along with Billie Holiday on the radio. Or maybe it was Johnny Cash, she isn't sure. As she thinks about it, she isn't sure about any of the details. She can't remember what her mother was wearing, whether she was thin or fat, how she wore her hair, in a bun or down around her face. She can't remember what her mother looked like before the illness. Hard as she tries, she can't conjure up her face. It's slipping away already. She knows there will come a day when she doesn't miss her mother anymore—a day when she only misses the feeling of missing. But she's not there yet. She still feels something of the dead hovering inside of her. It lives for a moment in her chest, misshapen and bruised as a backyard fruit. She closes her eyes and lets it hang inside of her. Then it falls away, too heavy to hold. She starts up the engine and heads on toward home.

2. PEACHES IN WINTER

Yvette smells what's happening under the table, but she doesn't say anything. It doesn't seem appropriate to mention, given the circumstances. Nobody else says a word either. They just eat their food in silence. A new one floats up, and Yvette tries to hold her breath as she takes another bite of chicken. It's more difficult than she imagined, to eat without breathing.

Yvette's mother died yesterday. She died quietly, all drugged up, in a white room surrounded by a bevy of nurses from the Islands. It was a planned death, like a planned pregnancy. Everybody had plenty of time to mourn before the official end. Relatives from both sides have come to town for the funeral, which will be held tomorrow, and the aura at the table now is one of suppressed relief, and impatience for the ceremony to be over.

The last time Yvette saw her mother was two weeks ago in the hospice in New Haven. Her breasts were gone and she wore a kerchief on her head, so that she looked like a young boy. Her skin seemed to grow darker the closer she got to the other side, as if she was turning to wood before Yvette's very eyes. She drifted in and out of awareness, but when she was awake, all she could talk about was peaches: the swirling blush of them, the sweetness of them, the coolness of them, the roughness of the pit against her tongue. Yvette went all around New Haven that cold gray day looking for peaches, but they were out of season and when she came back to the hospice her mother was not talking about peaches anymore. Her eyes were closed and it was time to catch the bus back to campus.

A new smell wafts up from under the table. It's unbelievable that such a small dog could make such a big impact on the world. Yvette holds a napkin over her mouth and eyes the other guests. They scrape at their plates unhappily.

"Pass the yams, Yvette," her father says, nodding his big head toward the bowl. He looks fatter than he did two weeks ago. The weight sits on his chest, where it's supposed to be most deadly. She hands him the yams.

Aunt Grace made all the food. She and Uncle Byron drove all the way up from the city this morning with a whole trunkload of steamy Tupperware.

"Have you chosen a major?" Byron asks her from across the table.

"English. Literature."

"Uh-oh, you know what that means, James," he says. "She'll

be moving back home after graduation." He snorts with laughter. "All these liberal arts kids do nowadays."

The thought of moving back here after college has filled her mouth with the taste of metal. She takes a sip of sweet tea, trying to wash it away.

Through the window above Byron's head, she can see it has begun to snow. Soft flakes drift down and make a home on the branches of the oak tree where she used to sit, hiding from the world. She went there for many reasons, but the one she remembers most is her father. Once it was the pig's feet that made him angry. He had decided she was too skinny, had become obsessed with this fact, and on one of the nights her mother was working late, he had fixed pig's feet for her dinner. She grew nauseated by its smell before it even hit the plate, and refused to eat. While he hovered over her, she'd taken a first bite, then gagged and spit it out. He tried to force the same half-chewed piece back into her mouth but she squirmed out of his grip and ran outside. She made it up the oak tree before he could catch her.

Another fart floats up just then, a real doozy. Aunt Grace coughs into her napkin.

"Goddamn it," her father says, rising. His chair falls to the floor behind him. "Where is that fucking dog?"

He reaches under the table and she hears a yelp as Teddy is dragged from his hiding place. Teddy is old, nearly toothless. Named for Teddy Pendergrass, he was her mother's dog, a replacement baby for when Yvette got too old to hold, and she used to take him everywhere. Now he sleeps almost all the time. Her father grips the dog by the scruff of his neck and belts him once, twice across his rump. The dog scurries away whimpering, his tail between his legs.

Her father picks up his fallen chair, looks down at the table, daring anybody to say a word.

Byron snorts with laughter. "I thought it was you all that time, James."

Aunt Grace chuckles a little and everybody goes back to their food.

Except Yvette. She stares out the window, where the snow is falling harder. When she was a kid, Yvette used to play a game at dinner: She would imagine she was a passerby on the street out front, somebody who just happened to glance in through their picture window at this dinner scene. She would imagine herself and her family through that stranger's eyes: a bespectacled, light-skinned man with a goatee, a slim, nervous brown-skinned woman serving food, a pudgy preteen girl in cornrows feeding scraps to the dog under the table. Would they see this scene and think, *Happy Family? The American Dream?* Would they see this scene as evidence of progress? Would they think, how wonderful, a black family living in this neighborhood? Or would they understand that the father, the good doctor, wore two faces. A healer by day could become cruel by night, wounding with the scotch flowing through his veins. Would they know just from looking that some nights after dinner, his tirades ended with her mother weeping, wishing aloud that she was dead? He never struck her with his fist, but he didn't have to. He was a genius at finding the right words to make her wish she'd never been born. On those nights, Yvette would lie in the dark, holding her pillow and praying to some faceless preacher God that her mother not die at her own hand. She never guessed her mother's death would come from the inside out—a passing of the most pedestrian and blameless variety.

— ◆ —

Yvette lies in the dark of her bedroom staring at the embers of her teenaged self. A poster of Michael Jackson still hangs above her bed, another of Jennifer Beals from *Flashdance* beside her dresser mirror. Her stomach makes unhappy sounds. Grace's chicken isn't sitting well with her, but somehow she drifts off to sleep.

She wakes sometime later in the darkness, to the sound of beeping garbage trucks outside.

Her mother looked almost beautiful in that hospice bed, androgynous and tiny, like a dark, fragile doll imported from a distant land. The last thing she said to Yvette: "What I wouldn't do for a peach."

Yvette gets up and goes to the bathroom off the hall with the framed sign on the wall that reads GOD BLESS THIS HOME. It's only 4:45 a.m. She heads back to her room, but instead of getting into bed she dresses in the dark, then goes outside and sits in her father's Volvo with the motor running, letting it warm up before she rolls slowly out of the driveway.

Connecticut is an embalmed state. The houses sit like taxidermy, their marble eyes watching her as she cruises past. The Stop & Shop is open, although the parking lot is empty. She doesn't know if it's been open all night or has just now opened for the morning. A man stands behind a table, under a sign that says ENSURE: COMPLETE, BALANCED NUTRITION FOR A HEALTHIER YOU. Behind him is a sculpture of bottles with the same words on them. When she moves past, he holds up a Dixie cup with white fluid in it. "Want some?" She takes the cup and sips from it. The drink tastes like chalk. It reminds her of the hospice, the fluids that flowed in and out of her mother. She hands it back, wipes her lip, and moves on toward the produce department.

The fruit is piled neatly, identical apples and identical pears, not a mark on their waxy skins. There are peaches too, imported from Chile at $2.99 a pound. She fills a bag with five of the heaviest, ripest ones she can find.

Outside, the sky has begun to brighten. She sits in the Volvo with the motor running, holding a peach. It's perfectly round and perfectly soft, but when she takes a bite, it doesn't taste sweet. It is a mealy, tasteless thing, and after a few nibbles, she sets it on the seat next to her.

She remembers that afternoon so many years ago, when her mother came home to find Yvette perched in the tree, still hiding from her father and his pig's feet. Her mother put her hands on her hips and laughed at the sight. "Is that a monkey I see up there?" she called up. "Come on down, sugar, I need your help."

That evening, Yvette sat at the kitchen table and shucked corn and watched her mother move around, cooking food Yvette wanted to eat and humming along with Stephanie Mills on the radio. Or maybe it was Patsy Cline. She isn't sure. As she thinks about it, she isn't sure about any of the details. She can't remember what her mother was wearing, whether she was thin or fat, how she wore her hair, in an Afro or braids. She can't remember what her mother looked like before the illness. Hard as she tries, she can't conjure up her face. It's slipping away already. She knows there will come a day when she doesn't miss her mother anymore—a day when she only misses the feeling of missing. But she's not there yet. She still feels something of the dead hovering inside of her. It lives for a moment in her chest, misshapen and bruised as a backyard fruit. She closes her eyes and lets it hang inside of her. Then it falls away, too heavy to hold. She starts up the engine and heads on toward home.

3. Plums in Winter

Soledad smells what's happening under the table, but she doesn't say anything. It doesn't seem appropriate to mention, given the circumstances. Nobody else says a word either. They just eat their food in silence. A new one floats up, and Soledad tries to hold her breath as she takes another bite of the honey-baked ham. It's more difficult than she imagined, to eat without breathing.

Soledad's mother died yesterday. She died quietly, all drugged up, in a white room surrounded by soft-spoken Filipina nurses. It was a planned death, like a planned pregnancy. Everybody had plenty of time to mourn before the official end. Relatives from both sides have come to town for the funeral, which will be held tomorrow, and the aura at the table now is one of suppressed relief, and impatience for the ceremony to be over.

The last time Soledad saw her mother was two weeks ago, in the hospice in New Haven. Her breasts were gone and she wore a Yankees cap on her head, so that she looked like a young boy. Her blue eyes looked hard as marbles, a doll's eyes that rolled back in her head when she writhed on the bed. She drifted in and out of awareness, but when she was awake, all she could talk about were plums, their blue-red skin, their sweet messiness, their coolness, the flat smoothness of the pit against her tongue. She talked about how there was no other word to describe their color but the name itself. Plum. Wasn't that remarkable? Soledad went all over New Haven that cold gray day looking for plums, but they were out of season, and when she came back to the hospice her mother was not talking about plums anymore. Her eyes were closed and it was time to catch the train back to campus.

A new smell wafts up from under the table. It's unbelievable that such a small dog could make such a big impact on the world. Soledad holds a napkin over her mouth and eyes the other guests. They scrape at their plates unhappily.

"Pass the macaroni, Soledad," her father says, nodding his big head toward the bowl. He looks fatter than he did two weeks ago. The weight sits in his bulbous belly, like a phantom pregnancy. She passes him the macaroni.

Aunt Rose made all the food. She and Uncle Izzy drove down from Boston this morning with a whole trunkload of steamy Tupperware.

"Have you chosen a major?" Izzy asks her from across the table.

"Women's studies," she says.

"Uh-oh, Dave," Izzy says, smirking at her father. "Sounds like trouble. Should have sent her down south for college."

She wants to say to him what she has learned, none of it in class: Some women are born to play dumb, and some women are too smart for their own good. Some women are born to give and some women only know how to take. Some women learn who they want to be from their mothers, some who they don't want to be. Some mothers suffer so their daughters won't. Some mothers love so their daughters won't. She wants to tell him that she has lost the one thing tying her to this scene. That nothing binds her to this anymore. That she is light and she is free and she is mourning not just her mother but her prison too.

Instead she forces a smile at him and sips her water.

Through the window above Izzy's head, she can see it has begun to rain. The wetness creates a kind of Impressionist haze that she finds comforting. She can make out through the wet half darkness the branches of the apple tree where she used to sit as a kid, hiding from the world. She went there for many reasons, but the one she remembers best is her father. The first time it happened, when she was twelve, she got out of school early for some reason and came home unannounced—came home to hear music playing, old soul music, in the middle of the afternoon. Confused, curious, she went toward the source, her father's office. The door was cracked open. The girl had black ringlets and high yellow skin and looked like a student, in faded jeans, an army jacket. Her backpack was in the middle of the floor, on the Persian rug, and she was sitting on his lap, laughing. Her father was speaking in a kind of affected slang she'd never heard before: "Why you been playing hard to get?" And the girl was saying, also in forced slang, "You have quite a reputation, Professor-man." Then their private laughter. Soledad turned and walked outside, her cheeks burning and her head down as if she'd been chastened. She climbed the tree and waited among the branches for the girl to leave and the house to become her house again. When the sky had turned a swirl of purple and gray and the air began to smell of burning wood, the girl emerged out the side door looking younger and a little unsteady, like a version of Soledad herself. She walked toward a beat-up Toyota halfway down the block and then she was gone.

Another fart floats up just then, a real doozy. Aunt Rose coughs into her napkin.

"Goddamn it, now that's enough," her father says, standing. His chair falls to the floor behind him. "Where is that thing?"

He reaches under the table and she hears a yelp as Blue is dragged from his hiding place. Blue is old, nearly toothless. He was her mother's dog, a replacement baby for when Soledad got too old to hold, and she took Blue everywhere. Now he sleeps almost all the time. Her father grips the dog by the scruff of the neck and belts him once, twice across his rump. The dog scurries away, whimpering, his tail between his legs.

Her father picks up his fallen chair, looks down at the table, daring anybody to say a word.

Izzy snorts with laughter. "I thought it was you all that time, Melvin."

Aunt Rose chuckles a little and everybody goes back to their food.

Except Soledad. She stares out the window, where the rain is falling harder. When she was a kid, Soledad used to play a game at dinner: She would imagine she was a passerby on the street out front, somebody who just happened to glance in through their picture window at this dinner scene. She would imagine herself and her family through that stranger's eyes: a portly black man at the head of the table, a white red-haired woman in a peasant blouse serving food from the kitchen, a yellow teenaged girl with corkscrew curls feeding scraps to the dog under the table. Would they guess the good professor, with all his Poitier dreams, was living a double life? Would they see the duplicity behind his smile? Would that stranger understand that this was not the revolution they had been waiting for, not the fulfillment of some folk-song plea? Would they see the daughter's burden of too much information? She always smiled hard and wide on Picture Day, so wide her jaw hurt a little, hoping that her smile could keep calamity at bay—hoping to keep her mother's innocence intact and the picture of the patchwork family intact. And maybe it worked, because somehow her parents stuck together, started to look a little alike. And in the end, her parents' parting came from the inside out—an ending of the most pedestrian and blameless variety.

———◆◆◆———

Later, Soledad lies in the dark of her bedroom staring at the embers of her teenaged self. A poster of Public Enemy still hangs above her bed, another of Jennifer Beals from *Flashdance* beside her dresser mirror. Her stomach makes unhappy sounds. Aunt Rose's ham isn't sitting well with her, but somehow she drifts off to sleep.

She wakes sometime later in the darkness to the sound of beeping garbage trucks outside.

Her mother looked almost beautiful in that hospice bed, androgynous and finally thin, the girl-woman a thousand diets had failed to make her. The last thing she said to Soledad: "What I wouldn't do for a nice cold plum."

Soledad gets up and goes to the bathroom off the hall with the puffy pink toilet seat that makes a sighing noise when she sits down on it. It's only 4:30 a.m. She heads back to her room, but instead of getting back into bed she dresses in the dark, then goes outside and sits in her father's Subaru with the motor running, letting it warm up before she rolls slowly out of the driveway.

Connecticut is an embalmed state. The houses sit like taxi-dermy, their marble eyes watching her as she cruises past. The Star Market is open, although the parking lot is empty. She doesn't know if it's been open all night or has just now opened for the morning. A man stands behind a table, under a sign that says ENSURE: COMPLETE, BALANCED NUTRITION FOR A HEALTHIER YOU. Behind him is a sculpture of bottles with the same words on them. When she moves past, he holds up a Dixie cup with white fluid in it. "Would you like to try Ensure?" She stares into the cup, always tempted by free lunches, but it reminds her of the hospice. She shakes her head and moves on toward the produce department.

The fruit is piled neatly, identical apples and identical pears, not a mark on their waxy skins. There are plums too, imported from Ecuador at $3.99 a pound. They are mostly hard, gold still showing under the purple. She fills a bag with six of the ripest she can find.

Outside, the sky has begun to brighten. She sits in the Subaru with the motor running, eating a plum. It doesn't taste sweet or messy. It is a hard, clean, bitter thing, and after a few tries, she sets it on the seat next to her.

She remembers that afternoon so many years ago, when her mother came home to find Soledad in the tree, still hiding from her true father. Her mother put her hands on her hips and laughed at the sight. "Is that a monkey up there?" she called up. "Come on down, babe, I need your help."

That evening, Soledad sat at the kitchen table and chopped collard greens and watched her mother move around, cooking dinner, cheerful and oblivious, humming along with Karen Carpenter on the radio. Or maybe it was Joni Mitchell, she isn't sure. As she thinks about it, she isn't sure about any of the details. She can't remember what her mother was wearing, whether she was thin or fat, how she wore her hair back then, in a braid down her back or frizzed up and wild around her face. She can't remember what her mother looked like before the illness. Hard as she tries, she can't conjure up her face. It's slipping away already. She knows there will come a day when she doesn't miss her mother anymore—a day when she only misses the feeling of missing. But she's not there yet. She still feels something of the dead hovering inside of her. It lives for a moment in her chest, misshapen and bruised as a backyard fruit. She closes her eyes and lets it hang inside of her. Then it falls away, too heavy to hold. She starts up the engine and moves toward the road. It is still wide open.

· What's the Matter with Helga and Dave? ·

When I married Hewitt, I didn't realize—among other things—that I would become a member of that mewling and defensive group of people known as Interracial Couples. And who could fault them their mewling? Everywhere I went with Hewitt, strangers commented—in subtle and not so subtle ways—on the fact of our unlikely union: me, a white woman, married to him, a black man.

The world, it seemed, though not united in their opinion of our kind, was united in their *awareness* of our kind, and by extension, their need to remark upon it—the fact of me, a white woman, married to him, a black man.

The only problem, of course, was that it wasn't true. Any of it.

I was not a white woman and Hewitt was not a black man— at least not technically speaking. We were both of mixed heritage. That is, we each had one white parent and one black parent. And we'd each come out with enough features of one parent to place us in different categories. Hewitt had come out looking to the world like a black man, and I'd come out looking to the world like a white woman, so when we got together, it was like we were repeating our parents' history all over again. We were supposed to be the next generation, all newfangled and melting-potted, but instead we were like Russian nesting dolls. When you opened our parents' bodies you found a replica of their struggle, no matter how hard we tried to transcend it.

In any case, I was passing and Hewitt was passing when we moved into the Chandler that July.

Did I mention I was nine months' pregnant with our first child? I was huge, but I felt strangely light, as if I was floating in water all the time. Pregnancy was a state of permanent romance. I was waiting, breath held, to meet the great love of my life. We both were. We held hands everywhere we went, me a white woman, him a black man.

The Chandler stood out on that strip of beautiful old buildings. It had been built a year before we moved in, despite protests from the old guard who said it was tacky, would ruin the row of otherwise historical buildings from the Golden Age of Hollywood, buildings that had housed the likes of Mae West, Ava Gardner, and Cary Grant. The Chandler was ugly and new and sat at the edge of the country club, with a banner in front that read NOW LEASING—THE CHANDLER—AN ELEGANT APART-

MENT ENCLAVE. As you walked up the ramp to the building, another sign, smaller, encouragingly said, *You're Almost Home!*

The people who lived in the Chandler were an odd assortment, every variation you could think of on new money: yuppies and film executives and starlets-in-training and people awaiting renovations on their houses in the hills and foreign businessmen who must have liked the sterility and convenience of hotel living. I'd been drawn to the cleanliness and orderliness of the building and the apartment, the gleaming new washer and dryer, the stainless-steel stove and refrigerator. I knew that motherhood would bring plenty of mess—shit and spit-up, diapers piled up to the ceiling, stretch marks. The old me would have wanted to live somewhere crumbling and old, with the charm of gilded-era Hollywood. The new me wanted a sleek, modern hotel suite with centralized air-conditioning and no history and no dirt.

It was only after we moved into the Chandler that I noticed all the interracial couples traversing the halls and loitering around the coffee machine.

The building manager herself was in that group—a plump Italian-American girl from Queens who had somehow landed in Los Angeles. She was married to a guy I only ever knew as Dude, a short black man with a Mighty Mouse physique and a high, soft, girlish voice like Mike Tyson's. They had a child together, a very pretty two-year-old monster named Gregoriah. Hewitt and I blanched every time Gregoriah happened to get on the elevator with us. Usually it meant we were going no-where, as he would lie down halfway in and halfway out of the elevator, his arms and legs splayed out, laughing, while the doors stayed open and the elevator stayed still and one of his parents tried to coax him on or off the thing.

Then there were Patricia and Tibor. Patricia was a svelte brown-skinned black woman in her sixties with the fading glam-our of a retired actress. Tibor was her Hungarian husband, a lawyer in his seventies who was built like a snowman—a belly that jutted out as far as mine did during that long, hot final month of my pregnancy.

And then there was the couple down the hall, Helga and Dave. For months Dave remained a shadowy figure. I'd catch a glimpse of his big bright smile and shellacked brown skin oc-casionally on the local morning news, as he interviewed a lion trainer or stood at the base of a mud slide in a fancy suit. But I rarely saw him in the halls of the Chandler, and when I did he would offer his newscaster's accentless and cheery "Hello!" and little else.

It was his wife, Helga, whom I got to know that fall at the Chandler—and it is Helga I think about whenever I drive by that building now, looking somehow still gleaming and new on that old and winding road.

—◆—

It was a week after I gave birth, when I was a battered and swollen mess, that I first saw Helga. I had big plans that day to go for a walk with George, who was still tiny and otherworldly, not altogether human. It was the first time either of us had left the apartment since we'd come home from the hospital. I made it as far as the sidewalk in front of the Chandler. The cars on Rossmore Avenue were speeding past and the sun beat down from a cloudless sky and I stood with my hands on the stroller, unable to continue. George, asleep in his pram, looked too tiny and too new for such a world. I turned around and went back inside.

It was in the elevator going up that I first laid eyes on her, pale, emaciated, stern-faced, in dark jeans and sunglasses. I glanced in her stroller and took note of the baby's brown skin and corkscrew black curls. She looked only a few months old, but I could not imagine that the mother—with her svelte shape and placid expression—had ever carried a child inside her, much less pushed one out.

The woman glanced at George and me without much interest but didn't say a word.

A week later, while out on a walk with Hewitt and George, I saw the woman again, but she was without the baby, and this time—after looking back and forth between my face and Hewitt's—her face broke into an excited smile. She said, "You're one of us!"

I nodded, and said, "Yes, we live in the Chandler too."

She introduced herself as Helga. This time, she peered into

the pram at George and proclaimed him adorable, winking up at me as if we were members of the same elite club.

The next day I found a gift for George on the doorstep—a tiny pair of UGG boots, the trendy shearling ones made for skiers that all the starlets in Los Angeles liked to wear with microminiskirts on ninety-degree days. There was a note attached: *Welcome to the Chandler! We are so thrilled to have you as our neighbors. Drinks? Dinner? Soon! Helga and Dave.*

I tried the boots on George. They fit okay, but he was wearing only diapers, and when I brought him into the living room to show Hewitt, he said, "He looks like a member of the Village People," and made me take them off.

—◦◆◦—

I was living on no sleep. George woke every two hours to feed on my sore and chafing breasts.

Hewitt, in a gesture of solidarity, insisted on getting up in the middle of the night with me, and so we began our ritual of sitting up together in the dark on the sofa in front of the flickering television while I nursed the baby.

We discovered that Nick at Nite was running what they called "Huxtapalooza"—back-to-back episodes of *The Cosby Show*. Hewitt and I both hated *The Cosby Show*, with venom and vigor—for its smugness, for the cloying sweetness of the vignettes pretending to be plots, for the surrealism of a rich black family who had no problem integrating into white America.

And yet in those early weeks after the birth, we watched it

every night in drop-jawed stultification, our baby suckling away at my sore bosom. I think now, looking back on it, we were in some strange way defending our right to exist as a well-to-do black family—because the world outside our door, in that strange, tilted, black-and-white cookie of a universe that was the Chandler, insisted we were just another interracial couple with a butterscotch baby in a $700 pram. The world out there insisted that as soon as a black man made it, he should marry a white woman. As soon as a black woman made it, she should marry a white man. But at night, in the privacy of our lair, we were that strange rare bird called a black family that squawked and flitted across the screen for a festival and was gone.

Of all the characters, I hated Claire Huxtable the most—a black woman lawyer who had five children and no trouble making it as a partner in an old boys' firm. Hewitt hated Denise the most. The actress was mixed, like us. Something about her bone-pale pallor and drugged-out eyes unsettled him, he said. That first night, we watched the episode where Cliff makes Theo return a pricey designer shirt, and Denise agrees to sew him a replica that turns out to be a disaster. Hewitt, beside me on the couch, shook his head and said in a fake southern accent, "Sometimes when y'all mix you come out real pretty—but sometimes y'all come out real fucked up."

George was asleep and we should have gone to bed, but we couldn't tear our eyes away.

The next episode was the one where Cliff's parents celebrate their forty-ninth anniversary. As a gift, the family commissions a painting from a photograph of the couple, and performs a dance and lip-synching performance to Ray Charles's "(Night Time Is) The Right Time."

Afterward, in bed, I spooned Hewitt from behind. It had begun to rain outside, and I saw through the window the glittering lights on Rossmore, and could hear the sound of the cars moving through the wet night. George was asleep in the pram next to me. Two years earlier I had been single and lonely and working as a graphic designer for a magazine in New York. It was a job and a life I'd been happy to walk away from. I had a pleasant feeling of surprise as I took stock of my life, as if I'd gotten away with something.

----◦◆◦----

That fall there were reports in the Metro Region section of the *Los Angeles Times* about a spate of racial incidents in the Brentwood public schools.

Hewitt told me about the latest incident over breakfast.

"Some white kids called their black substitute teacher an 'N-word,'" Hewitt said. "The kids got suspended but now the parents are protesting, saying that their kids did nothing wrong."

I stared down at my baby's face. He was in what they called "the fourth trimester"—not yet fully of this world. His eyes were gray and looked almost blind. I wondered what he could see, if he could make out shapes or colors or features, or if I was still just a smell and a taste to him.

I shook my head. "They called the teacher a nigger? What's the world coming to?"

"No, not a nigger," Hewitt said. "They called him an N-word."

"I don't understand."

Hewitt put down the paper and picked up his coffee and said, "Literally. They said, 'Hey, N-word!' Not 'Hey, nigger.' 'Hey, N-word!'"

Helga invited me to take a walk with her and her baby that week and I agreed readily. Hewitt was spending several days a week at the university and I was alone with George for the first time and eager for adult companionship.

To the world we passed on those city streets we must have looked like two wealthy white women out with their mixed babies. And in a funny way, to a passerby Helga must have appeared the blacker of us two, by association at least. Gia with her dark skin and corkscrew curls was a clear giveaway that Helga had—as Hewitt put it—"the fever for the flavor."

Somewhere on that long walk, Helga leaned her head into George's stroller and shook her head at the sight of his pale skin and flaxen hair. "He's so fair. I would never know."

"Never know?"

"I mean, he's not like Gia, where you can just tell immediately." Helga looked between the two babies and sighed. "Well, it doesn't matter. They are both perfect. Mixed kids are the prettiest, aren't they?" She started down the street but I stood where I was for a moment, watching her rail-thin behind swishing away.

"Well, George is not mixed, I mean not really," I said, catching up with her. I waited for her to ask what I meant so that I could explain. But she didn't ask. She just laughed and said, "Come on, look at him. He's a blondie!"

I was about to clarify when she leaned into his pram and said, "Hi, Blondie!" and George said, "Hi!" back.

Helga glanced at me, suspicious, as if she thought I was throwing my voice.

I shrugged, laughed. "Isn't that funny?" I said. "He says that whenever we lean into his pram to say hi."

It was true. George had been doing it since he was two weeks old. Whenever we leaned into his pram or his crib and said "Hi," he would say "Hi!" back. Hewitt insisted I was hearing things, but it happened consistently enough that I knew it was really "Hi!" he was saying.

I leaned in to show Helga.

"Hi!" I said.

"Hi!" George said.

I clapped and laughed and we did the routine again.

Helga stepped away from the pram, grim-faced, and shook her head. "You shouldn't clap at his tricks as if he is a monkey. You must ignore it if it happens again."

"Why?"

"Why?" She stared at me for a moment, her mouth set into

a straight, firm line. "American mothers," she said, "they turn their babies into dolls. Chimps. In Germany we are more nonchalant. We don't hover, we don't smother our babies. I leave Gia alone on a rug most of the time. I let her figure things out on her own. She doesn't need me getting in the way of her learning process. You understand?"

I nodded, a little taken aback by the harshness of her tone.

Helga took off her sunglasses and stared at me as if she was trying to decide something about me. From the pram I could hear George saying "Hi!" over and over again, as if daring me to look at him. Helga pretended not to hear him, so I did too.

"I have a book for you," she said. "I will give it to you when we get home."

Sure enough, she left it on our doorstep later that evening with a Post-it attached that said, *For your interest.*

It was slim, more a pamphlet than a book, and showed a photograph of a woman with long, dark hair, smiling and leaning over a baby on the floor. The baby—in a simple white onesie—was kicking its bare legs and clapping, but not smiling. There was a disconnected feeling to the two figures, as if they'd been cut from separate photographs and pasted together.

The book's title was *Dear Mother: Treating Your Baby with Respect.*

I read it in bed while George slept. The writing was awkward and reminded me of a Dianetics pamphlet I'd once been handed on a subway platform. The gist of the book was that you should not treat your infant like a baby. You should talk to your baby in full sentences and in an adult tone of voice. You should tell your infant that you are going to pick him up before you do it and that you are going to change his diaper before you do it. You should not speak to your baby in a shrill or condescending voice, should not clap for your baby, and should never say "good boy" or "good girl" to your baby. Most of the time you should leave your baby alone on the floor, thus not interfering with his self-motivated learning process. The author had developed the philosophy while she worked at a Romanian orphanage.

———— ·◆· ————

"Hogwash," Hewitt said as he stepped out of the bathroom, holding the book in his hand. He'd been locked in there for the past twenty minutes reading it on the toilet. "This is complete bunk, and written by illiterates to boot. Tell your fräulein friend that we don't need her parenting advice, thank you. If George wants to say 'Hi,' and if George wants to say 'Back off, bitch,' and if George wants to say 'Kiss my black—yes, black—ass,' we're going to cheer and laugh like any normal motherfucking parents. You don't create an authentic baby by acting fake."

"That's what I thought," I said.

Hewitt tossed the book on the floor and threw his body down on the bed beside me.

"But by the way, sweetie," he said, in a gentle voice he used when he was about to piss me off. "I hate to tell you this, but

George didn't really say, 'Hi.' You've got to stop insisting on that. It just makes you sound crazy."

"He did too."

"Did not."

"Did too."

"Did not."

"Did too."

We watched *Cosby* that night in stony silence.

The Huxtapalooza festival was in its second week. The episode that night centered on Sondra, the pale-as-a-bedsheet eldest daughter, and her elfin boyfriend with the unfortunate name Elvin. Sondra gets into a fight with Elvin and breaks up with him, and Cliff tries to set her up with an upstanding young man he seems to have his own crush on, but Sondra has no eyes for the new guy.

Hewitt tried to make conversation by pointing out to me that the new guy on the date with Sondra was the same actor who returns in a later season to play Denise's husband.

"Isn't that weird—that they cast the same guy in two different roles, as the love interest of two different daughters, and never acknowledge it? Like we're going to forget that horse face."

George was asleep on my breast and we were free to go to bed, but we stayed up to watch the next episode because Hewitt had seen it before and promised me it would be of "personal interest" to me.

It turned out to be the episode where Theo's college archaeology professor leads a class discussion about the diverse ethnic backgrounds of the Egyptians, and as an example, encourages the students to guess her own heritage.

The students shout out their guesses. "Italian!" "Greek!" "Irish!"

"N-word," Hewitt muttered beside me.

Sure enough, the woman reveals to the class that she is part black: Irish, Cherokee, and black. Later, she goes over to the Huxtables' house to try to convince Cliff and Claire to let Theo go on a class dig in Egypt that summer. Theo makes the whole family gather around the professor—aptly named Professor Grayson—and guess her ethnicity. Everybody guesses wrong and when Theo tells them the truth, they stare at her with a kind of gleaming-eyed hunger, like they're going to cook her on a spit, or at least ask her to play one of their daughters.

I put George in his bassinette beside the bed and got into bed. Hewitt rolled over and kissed me and said he was sorry he had been so gruff earlier.

"Maybe George really did say 'Hi,'" he offered. "What do I know?"

We kissed and said, "I love you." Still, afterward, in the dark, I felt a distance between us I couldn't properly explain.

——— ◆ ———

Helga left a note on our door a few days later. *Dinner? You and Hewitt? This Friday at seven?*

I convinced Hewitt we should go. He knew I was lonely and needed to make friends with other mothers.

When I called Helga to confirm, she sounded pleased. "Oh, and you can leave George at your place with the baby phone."

"The baby phone?"

"What is the word for it?" she said. "You know—the monitor! The monitor. Leave him at your place with the monitor. We only live a few doors down, so you should get reception."

I felt my mouth go dry. "I don't think—"

She sighed. "Okay, bring him. I mean, whatever you're comfortable with. But at some point he will need to learn to be by himself."

When Friday night rolled around, I didn't dare tell Hewitt what Helga had suggested. He already seemed irritated enough. He came out of our room sighing and unshowered, wearing rumpled blue jeans and a polo shirt. His hair was wild, overgrown. I considered asking him to change outfits or fix his hair, but his expression was so sullen I thought better of it.

I had tried my hardest to look nice in a blue wraparound dress from J.Crew that still fit me, but I felt frumpy in it. None of my other prepregnancy clothes fit, and although my maternity clothes were too big, I still looked four months' pregnant. More than one smiling stranger on the street had asked me, "How many months along are you?"

Hewitt lugged a sleeping George down the hall in his car seat.

Helga and Dave's apartment was a more expensive model than ours—a model we'd looked at during our tour of the Chandler, just for kicks. Inside, the place looked like a nightclub, with dim lighting, thin hard furniture, no sign of a child's garish toys anywhere. Dave sat perched on a barstool wearing a blue dinner jacket, a crisp pink oxford shirt, and a pair of tight chinos. Helga wore a complicated silver sheath.

While Hewitt, still lugging George in the car seat, went to shake hands with Dave, Helga pulled me into Gia's room to show me the sleeping baby. I sensed that she really wanted me to see the nursery. And once inside, I could see why. It was perfect—the hip nursery for the hip mom, furnished by various French and Scandinavian companies. I'd trawled the Internet for weeks before George was born ogling these very items, but Hewitt had talked me out of spending our life's savings on baby gear. Instead our house was filled with the plastic degradation of Fisher-Price.

Helga pointed at Gia where she slept on her belly in a pair of white satin pajamas, an orange silk bandanna tied Aunt Jemima fashion in her hair. "This crib," Helga whispered as she pointed to her daughter, "it costs a fortune but it's so worth it. It converts to a toddler bed. You should buy one for George."

Gia shifted, moaned, and Helga hissed, "We'd better talk outside."

After she shut the door behind us, she said, "Gia cried for an hour last night. I think she has a cold, but we're sleep-training her, so I just let her cry it out. That child has lungs on her."

I had heard of this mythic sleep training crafted by a man named Ferber. But we were using the Cosby method: Watch Huxtapalooza all night, so that baby never misses you and you never miss baby.

I followed her into the kitchen and stood while she moved around putting food from the stove onto platters.

She handed me a glass of white wine.

"Have you found a nanny yet?" she asked.

"Actually, we're not sure we want one," I said. It was true. Hewitt and I had decided we didn't like the nanny culture in L.A.—all those shadowy Mexican women trudging along, pushing sullen white children. It was positively antebellum.

"You're very brave," Helga said. "I would just die without Teresa. I like being around Gia too, but not all the time. I mean, it's awfully difficult to get anything done. I have Gia in day care during the week, of course. It's wonderful. They let the babies hang out on the floor. But evenings and weekends I have Teresa."

I nodded. I had seen Gia with the woman, rolling around town. And now I watched Helga move around the immaculate kitchen, thin and angular in her silver sheaf, so elegant and rested, as if she had never given birth. There was something alarming about it to me, even as I half hungered to look that way too.

In the living room, Hewitt was rocking George's car seat with one hand and nursing a highball with the other. He nodded his head sympathetically while Dave, still perched on the stool, ranted, his smooth newscaster veneer gone and his face twisted with rage.

"It's outrageous," Dave was saying, "the way these people on the street act like they know everything about me, sucking their teeth, shaking their heads, sometimes even making comments under their breath. I don't even know these people! And they're judging me? Judging my choice for a wife? Judging my child? I mean, I've had people say, 'You must be into white women,' just because I'm married to Helga. '*Into white women.*' I mean, what does that even mean? Oh, it makes my blood boil."

"I hear you man, I hear you," Hewitt said. He gave me a sly smile and said, "I can relate," in an earnest voice I'd never heard him use before. He lifted his glass. "To a color-blind future."

"Right on," Dave said, and lifted his glass.

I looked at Hewitt, trying to figure out what he was up to, but he avoided my eyes and stared into his glass intently.

Over dinner, Dave was a good host, asking all the right newscastery questions of each of us about work and baby, laughing at the appropriate moments. George woke once for a feeding but otherwise dozed on the floor.

The food was rich beef stew that Hewitt had to beg off of since he didn't eat meat.

I guzzled it. I had given birth. I was nursing. I felt keenly my place in the animal kingdom.

At one point Dave began to talk about why he preferred Los Angeles to New York, where he and Helga had lived before. He said he hated the rats and the subway and the dark winter afternoons. He hated the claustrophobia of everybody living on top of everybody, and let's face it, he told us, he hated the filth.

"And I'll be honest with you, man," he said, looking at Hewitt, "I got tired of trying to catch a cab, you know what I mean?"

Hewitt emitted a little laugh. "Tell me about it. When we lived back East, I always used to have to send Rachel out to the curb ahead of me to nab one."

Dave laughed. "Me too! Helga was the bait. You should have seen the cabbies when they saw me coming up behind her." He looked at Helga and I sensed some ice behind his smile. "I try to explain to Helga but she's not American, so it goes right over her head."

Hewitt looked at me and grabbed my hand and said, in a saccharine voice, "I try to explain to Rachel too. Don't I, sweetie? She's an American and she still doesn't get it."

I looked at the faces around the table—Dave's big television smile and Helga's square face, which looked sad just then as she moved her stew around in the bowl without eating it.

Hewitt was smirking, enjoying himself—was he tipsy? He was playing a game and I knew he'd been playing it all evening. These people didn't know us. They only knew what they saw. I kicked what I hoped was Hewitt's shin under the table. "Yes," I said, "Hewitt tries to explain to me. I think I get it now. I think I'm finally beginning to understand what you all go through."

At the door, saying good-bye, I heard Dave saying to Hewitt, "It's so cool you guys are our neighbors. This building is full of us. Have you noticed? It's awesome."

I heard Hewitt give a strangled little laugh and say, "Yeah, we've noticed."

As soon as we were safely inside our apartment, I turned to Hewitt. "You dirty bastard, I saw what you did."

"You're pretty cute for a white girl," he said, heading down the hall with the car seat and George.

I followed him. "Now we have to tell them the truth some-how. I mean, we're going to see more of them."

"No we aren't. I can't hang out with that airhead. Did you hear him? 'Coat of many colors.' 'We are the world.' Ugh. TV. I hate TV people. Mediocre minds." He sat down on the couch and turned on the TV. The honorable doctor, Heathcliff Huxtable, was just stepping across the kitchen in another wacky sweater of bright geometric shapes.

George woke and began to whimper and flail his arms. I took him out of the car seat and put him on my lap and helped him latch onto my nipple. I realized only then that I'd been uncomfortable all night, a tension like a live wire running through my body. I felt better as soon as the baby made contact. I stared down at him, and I must have been a little drunk—or maybe it was the hormones—but my tears began to flow. They dropped onto the baby, who didn't notice. His eyes were closed as he suckled.

Hewitt beside me was fumbling for the remote control and talking to himself. "I hate this episode. Rudy breaks Cliff's new juicer with her fat white friend what's-his-name, Piggy or Peter or something. I hate it when it's all about kiddie stuff. Pudding commercial bullshit."

He switched channels then and suddenly we were watching *Good Times*. JJ gyrated across the screen to the wild hoots of the studio audience.

Hewitt chuckled. "Can you believe somebody as stone-cold ugly as JJ got all the girls? That was some old white man's practical joke." He began to rattle off trivia about the show. "And another thing, did you know that the actress playing the mother was seventeen years older than the dude playing the dad? That's some sick shit."

I was weeping beside him, silently, but he didn't notice. The baby was letting out little satisfied sighs and gulps at my breast. On-screen, Florida Evans had her hands on her hips and was saying something dignified and articulate to her brood of children.

On our next walk, Helga told me about her background. She came from poverty—a factory-worker father, a government-clerk mother. They'd lived in East Germany, where Helga pursued her ambition to be an Olympic gymnast. She trained night and day under the abusive regime of an ambition-crazed coach.

After a slip off the balance beam, she gave up her athletic career and went to university in Berlin. It was during a semester abroad in New York City that she'd met Dave.

"I never expected to stay in this country," Helga said, pausing on the sidewalk to pull a blanket over Gia. "I was only supposed to stay here a few years."

We were standing in front of a small stucco house that was being gutted. On the side where we stood, only the frame was left, so that we could look right inside to the dirt- and rubble-filled rooms. Mexican workmen moved in and out, carrying planks.

"Everything is temporary here," Helga said. "Everything is casual."

"Do you talk to your family much?"

"Every day," she said, starting to walk ahead.

"Do you get to visit them often?" I said, trailing behind her.

"No. I did when we lived on the East Coast. But L.A. is so much farther away. Everything is far away from here." Her voice had gone all thick, tremulous, and for a moment I thought she would cry. But when she looked back at me, her mouth was a straight line and her voice was clear again, her tone business-like. "Listen, I've been meaning to ask you. Do you want to share our nanny? We can share her."

"Share her?"

"A nanny share. Teresa needs extra hours," Helga said. "So I was thinking you could use her some of the week. I know you said you weren't sure you were going to get one—" She paused, laughed slightly. "But come on now. It's a necessity."

"I don't know," I said. "I'll have to talk to Hewitt."

The fact was, I was tempted. I had no time for myself—to think, to walk, and yes, to exercise or get my nails done. I was exhausted and sometimes I caught a glimpse of myself in a mirror and was startled. In my twenties, when I was single, I had vowed never to become weary and dumpy like the mothers I saw slumping around the city. I'd vowed never to give up on myself. But maybe I had. Even now, six weeks after the birth, I looked vaguely pregnant. My eyes were ringed with dark circles. My feet were thick and hard as horse's hooves—it had been so long since I'd had a pedicure. And my legs were hairy. Hewitt had run his hand along my leg in bed the other night and muttered, "It's Chewbacca, with a weave." Hewitt and I had not yet taken the leap to intercourse, and I felt anything but sexy.

———— • ◆ • ————

"She's gonna loan you her mammy?" Hewitt said, when I told him about Helga's proposition. "How generous of Miz Scarlett."

I explained to him how tired I was. I repeated a phrase Helga had said to me, word for word. "I need some time for myself. I'll be a better mother if I can have some time to take care of myself." I ran my hand along my leg. "Don't you want to see your wife again?"

Hewitt looked at my legs. "Hey, *Star Wars* was my favorite

movie." He sighed. "Okay. Whatever you want, babe. Let's get the mammy. What the hell."

Teresa was in her forties, with two children of her own, a broad smile, and a placid, matronly manner.

The first day she came, she took George for a walk while I wept on the bed and watched the clock. I went rushing to the door the minute I heard it open.

The next day I told Hewitt I feared George would grow to love Teresa more than me, she was so relaxed and bosomy and calm with him.

Hewitt shrugged. "So what? If that happens, we'll just fire her."

"But he'll miss her. We'll break his heart."

"Don't sweat it. By the time he's three he won't even remember her. He'll just have a vague sense of melancholia but he won't know what it's about."

"Thanks. I feel so much better."

On the third day I ventured out. I went to a salon down the street and got a haircut and an agonizing Brazilian bikini wax and a pedicure, and when I got home George was cooing on Teresa's broad lap, and I felt a whole lot better than I had in ages.

The day after that I went down to the gym and worked out for half an hour.

By the end of the week I felt one baby step closer to my old self.

That Saturday night, Hewitt and I had sex for the first time since I'd given birth. It was uncomfortable and strange, but not as painful as I'd feared. We took it slow, and afterward held each other in the dark and I felt I'd survived a car accident of epic proportions and was learning to walk again.

◆

A few weeks later, as I was taking a walk with George one afternoon, a woman, small and blond, came rushing up to me, smiling.

"Helga," she said in a slight accent.

I shook my head. "Sorry, you're mistaking me—"

She put a hand over her mouth. "I'm sorry. From a distance you looked so like her. I'm sorry." She glanced in at George in the pram, shook her head at her mistake, then slunk away.

It happened again a few days later.

A tan young man with blazing, professionally whitened teeth waved at me from the far end of the hallway in the Chandler.

I walked toward him, hesitantly smiling back, but as I got closer, his smile faltered and his teeth went away.

"Oops, from far away I thought you were that German girl," he said. "The light was behind you."

Hewitt, when I told him about the incidents, said it was ridiculous.

"You look nothing alike," he said, chuckling.

But then it happened again a week later.

It was the same small blond woman who'd mistaken me for Helga once before, but she was jogging and wearing a tracksuit and headphones. She ran past me in the parking lot of the Chandler, where Hewitt and I were loading the baby into the car, and she said something fast, in German. She was rushing and out of breath, and this time she didn't realize her mistake even when she got close enough to see my face. She just said something else in German, laughing, and then jogged past me out onto the street.

I got into the passenger seat beside Hewitt.

"Do you think it's because of the baby?" I said. "Do you think they see me with a black baby and assume I'm her?"

Hewitt shook his head. "Hon, hate to tell you this, but George doesn't exactly scream 'Africa.' He's like you, honey. And Gia's like me. Sometimes that's the way the cookie crumbles."

I looked back at him, a vague panic I couldn't explain building in my chest. "Well then, why? Why does it keep happening?"

Hewitt turned and looked at me, studied my face for a moment, and I couldn't tell what he was thinking. "I don't know."

The next time I took a walk with Helga, I looked at the babies side by side in their prams and saw Hewitt was right. They looked nothing alike. Mine looked like a Gerber baby, with golden-brown hair that twisted into a Tintin curl on the top of his head. His cheeks were huge and his skin was pale, and he was fat, with sausage-link arms and accordion legs. He had huge brown eyes and wore an expression of bewilderment. Helga's baby was brown-skinned and thin, with curly black hair and rather lanky limbs, a shrewd expression in her small dark eyes.

I eyed Helga's profile as we walked. She was much thinner than me, with a body that looked more suited for the runway than for childbirth. Her head was quite large and her features were angular, a series of straight lines and arrows. Helga wasn't pretty but she wasn't ugly either. My mother once told me men like women with big teeth. Helga's teeth were big. She looked around as we walked, with a mixture of boredom and hunger I'd seen on the faces of other Europeans.

I didn't think I looked like her, but suddenly I wasn't sure *what* I looked like. In a slight panic, I searched for a storefront, a car window, a reflective surface of any kind, but we were on a tree-lined street and all the cars were parked on the other side.

Beside me, Helga was telling me that Gia had recently said her first word. "She said 'Tata.'"

"What's that?"

"The nanny? Teresa? She calls Teresa 'Tata.'" She smiled. "Teresa was worried I'd be upset. She thought I'd be mad that she didn't say 'Mama' first."

"Were you?" I said, a pain spreading through my chest.

She scoffed. "God, no. It doesn't matter. I'd just die without Teresa. I wish I could keep her forever. Don't you just love her?"

"She's great," I said, though really I wasn't sure I liked the woman. Two days earlier I'd walked into the nursery and found her sitting in the rocking chair with George pressed against her bosom, snuggled there like it was home. She was trying to put him to sleep, just as she was supposed to do, but at the sight of them together, my stomach clenched up. I said George seemed hungry, though he didn't, and took him into the other room, where I nursed him to sleep.

From the pram, George began to whimper, and I was glad for the excuse to go home. "Well, I better get back and nurse him."

"You're still nursing him?" Helga said. "Let me give you some advice. Stop. I stopped after two months. They get all the benefits by then. It will really free you up."

"But I enjoy it. I mean, I like that I can do something special for him."

"You should see what it does to your breasts when you're done. Then you'll be sorry you didn't stop earlier."

———◆———

Helga invited me for walks a few more times, but I found ways to get out of it. I was tired. George was sick. I had work to do.

A few weeks went past without contact, and then one Sunday we saw Helga at the farmers' market.

I was wearing a polka-dotted sundress that hid my still-protruding belly. Hewitt was carrying George in the carrier on his chest, facing outward so that George could grin and wave and shout "Hi!" at all the people, as if he were a tiny mayor of the village.

"Hey, it's Eva Braun," Hewitt said, nodding in Helga's direction.

She was standing on the other side of the market next to her pram, chatting with the Frenchman who sold cheeses from around the world. She was wearing a shearling jacket, though the weather was balmy.

The market was packed with couples with young babies, each with a fancier stroller than the last. An African man with strange masklike features and a mop of mangled dreadlocks sat banging on a drum before an audience of sullen white toddlers. He wore a kente-cloth smock and cowrie beads and added an aura of hippie mayhem to the upscale faux-bohemian affair.

Hewitt pointed at him and whispered, "Check it out. That man's not really black. That's a dreadlock wig. And you can see the line of makeup on his neck."

Shocked, I squinted at the man. I edged a little closer, but I couldn't see what Hewitt was talking about. By the time I turned back to ask him, he had disappeared into the crowd of shoppers with George.

I forgot about the African man and settled into shopping, picking up berries, vegetables, olive bread, heirloom tomatoes, and a big bouquet of orange tulips.

I didn't see Hewitt again until I was almost at the other end of the horseshoe of produce vendors. He stood beside the Mango Man, his favorite vendor. He was talking to Helga. For a moment, I paused and watched them. She had taken off her shearling jacket in the heat and had hung it over the pram handle. Gia sat stone-faced and baking in a mini shearling coat that matched her mother's, surrounded by bags of fruit and vegetables. She was sucking furiously on her pacifier. Helga was wearing a sleeveless shirt and her bony shoulders looked almost translucent in the sunlight. She was laughing at something Hewitt was saying and throwing her head back so that the long expanse of her neck was exposed. I swallowed the sudden dryness in my throat. I edged closer. Hewitt was grinning and I heard him say, "So how did a beautiful woman like you get such an ugly name? Helga. Jeepers."

I couldn't believe the rudeness of the comment, but Helga was laughing as if it was the funniest thing she'd ever heard.

I cleared my throat and stepped forward. They both turned to look at me.

Helga eyed my dress with a slight twist of her mouth so that I knew it had been a mistake, that it made my belly look bigger, not smaller.

"Hello, Rachel," she said. "I didn't know you were here too."

"Where's Dave?" I asked, looking around for him.

"He's in San Francisco on work. Covering gas prices."

Hewitt was making George dance in the baby carrier for the benefit of passersby. He was holding George's arms out and making them move from side to side in an imitation of an Egyptian.

Helga leaned in and squeezed George's cheek and said, "Such a blondie!" Then, "Hewitt, you look good at putting things together. Are you handy?"

Hewitt shrugged. "I'm handy enough."

"I just bought this high chair from Sweden, and I can't figure out how to put the damn thing together. Dave's not coming back until later in the week and I wanted to feed Gia at the table like a big girl." She leaned into the pram and fingered Gia's curls. Gia made a deep growling sound in her throat but did not let the pacifier out of her mouth.

"Sure, I can come over later today. We don't have plans, do we, Rachel?"

I shook my head. "No plans."

"Great," Helga said. "Just come over sometime later today. Two-ish?"

"Two-ish," Hewitt said.

Helga waved good-bye and headed out of the market with Gia in tow. I watched her cross the street. She had parked her car in a handicap spot. There was a ticket on her windshield but she barely glanced at it as she went through the process of putting Gia and the vegetables into the back of the car. She drove off, with the parking ticket fluttering like a flag on her windshield.

We headed out of the market too, passing the African man, who was still drumming and wailing off tune. The crowd of toddlers had grown and they swarmed around him, picking up objects he had spread on a blanket before him—drums and bells and tambourines, along with a stack of CDs of his music. I slowed as we passed, trying to see if there was any truth to what Hewitt had said, but he was wearing a hat and his head was turned away, so it was impossible to tell.

———•◆•———

Back at the Chandler, Hewitt and I played with George for a while before putting him down for a nap. Hewitt made us goat-cheese-and-asparagus omelets that we ate in front of *Soul Train* reruns. After a while George woke up from his nap and I went to get him. When I returned to the living room, baby on my hip, Hewitt was in the bathroom. I sat on the sofa with George, waiting for Hewitt to come out of the bathroom. He wasn't making any noise in there and he didn't flush the toilet, but after a while he came out looking somehow refreshed. His features looked sharper, clearer, as if he'd wiped away a dirty film. He took George from me and held him in the air above his face and said, "I better go help Helga with that chair."

After he left, I sat watching the dance line on *Soul Train* while George lay on a blanket on the floor, shaking a rattle. He started to cry. I picked him up and put his face to my breast but he didn't seem hungry. I put him in his stroller and put on my sunglasses and jean jacket and headed out of the apartment for a walk. When I passed Helga's apartment, I slowed down. The door was shut. I paused. I could hear the muted bass of techno music, but when I stepped closer I wasn't sure it was coming from her place or from the apartment next door. I stood there, my ear to the door, until George squawked in the stroller and I pushed him fast toward the elevators.

Since it was a Sunday, the traffic on Rossmore was light. I made my way back toward the village, but when I saw it, on the other side of the big intersection, as the bustling yuppie enclave that it was, I decided against it. I went instead into a fast-food joint called Koo Koo Róo. It was full of thin white gay couples and robust Mexican families all enjoying their Sunday lunches. I stood there, trying to decide what I wanted. On the menu was an option where you could get three side dishes as a meal. I asked the girl behind the counter if I could make all three side dishes macaroni and cheese.

She shook her head. "What do you mean?"

I repeated myself. "Can I get option six, but make it all mac and cheese."

She shook her head. "I don't know what you're talking about."

I had to explain it to her two more times before she understood what I was asking for, and then she said she had to ask her manager.

Luckily her manager was standing beside her and he said to her, "Sure. Just press mac 'n' cheese three times when it asks for the options."

It turned out to be a lot of macaroni and cheese. I held my tray with the plate on it with one hand and pushed the stroller with the other and found a seat by the window. George was sucking on a frog toy and making cheerful noises. I didn't take off my jacket but sat hunched over the plate eating the macaroni and cheese with a plastic spork and watching the people outside the window going toward and away from the village. It seemed to me that half of the people I saw were interracial couples—not all black and white, but a mixture of mixes. I started to count them and got up to twelve when I realized my macaroni and cheese was gone.

Hewitt wasn't there when we returned, but George had fallen asleep in the stroller, so I left him by the door where it was dark and cool.

I sat in front of the television. *Dr. Phil* was on. The segment was about some obese woman whom they had to interview by satellite because she couldn't fit out the door. Her boyfriend was on the stage with Dr. Phil. He was an average-size guy who admitted to abusing the woman—kicking her in the stomach and pinching her and calling her a fat slob—even as he devoted his life to taking care of her.

Hewitt came home while I was watching. I didn't turn my head to see him. I kept my eyes on the show. Dr. Phil was explaining to the man that everyone deserves to be treated with dignity and respect. I heard Hewitt shut the door and pause at the stroller, put his keys down, walk toward me. I felt him watching me and tried to make my face go normal. Finally I turned to look at him.

He was wearing a different outfit than he'd been wearing when he left earlier. He was in gym shorts and a T-shirt and sneakers and he was all sweaty.

"I came back but you weren't here, so I decided to go work out," he said. "Where'd you guys go?"

"Koo Koo Roo. I was hungry." I watched him bend down to take off his sneakers. "When did you get back here?"

"It must have been a few minutes after you left," he said. "You should have waited for me."

"I didn't know how long you would take with the chair," I said.

"It was easy," he said. "I can't believe she couldn't put it together. It involved, like, a few screws and a wrench."

"Right."

"I'm going to take a shower before my BO kills you both."

"Okay."

George woke up while Hewitt was in the shower. I picked him up from his pram and on my way back to the living room saw that there was a small black gift bag from Barneys on the hall table beside Hewitt's keys. I'd somehow missed it when I came in. I picked it up and opened it. There were baby clothes inside. The bag, I saw now, was used—just something to put the clothes in. The clothes were used too—a worn T-shirt with the faded word ITALIA across it, and a knit sweater with geometric shapes on it, like something for a miniature Dr. Huxtable. Both smelled of old perfume and there was a slight yellow stain on the sweater, hidden in the shapes.

Hewitt's voice startled me. "Helga thought those might fit George."

I turned around to face him. He stood at the door to the living room, dripping from the shower, a towel around his waist. "They're too small for Gia," he said. "That girl's growing like a weed."

His words—"That girl's growing like a weed"—did not sound

like the Hewitt I knew, and I had the brief thought that he was different, that he had been replaced by somebody who looked just like him but was not him at all.

I swallowed. The light was coming in behind him, so I couldn't see his features, just the shape of him, his big head and broad shoulders and long legs.

"Anything nice?" he said, stepping toward me.

"No, just Eurotrash," I said, shifting George's weight on my hip. "Why did she think we'd want this junk? I've never seen Gia in clothes this ugly. I bet they aren't even hers."

"Oh," he said. He looked almost hurt by my comment. "She meant well, I'm sure."

I waited for him to tell a joke, something to make me feel right, but he was quiet, and a smell like rotten eggs floated up around us. I went to change George's diaper.

———— • ◆ • ————

It was eleven o'clock and we were reading in bed when the lightbulb on my nightstand flickered and went out. I got up and went into the kitchen to get a new bulb, and discovered it was the whole apartment that had gone dark. The power was out. And when I looked out the window, I saw that all the lights in all the apartment windows were out. Even the green neon sign atop the old building across the street was gone, disappeared into the blackness. Without light, the city became what it had always meant to be, a sea of cars in a desert of darkness.

"It's a blackout," I said to Hewitt, who had come to find me.

We stumbled around the kitchen searching for candles and flashlights.

"I guess this means no *Cosby* tonight," Hewitt said.

I stopped and looked at him. "Huxtapalooza's been over for weeks."

"Really?" He looked sincerely surprised.

"Why do you think we've been watching *Good Times*?"

He stared at me blankly, but before he could answer there was a knock on the door.

Hewitt headed down the hall with a flashlight and I heard the sound of the door opening and a woman's voice, a muted back-and-forth.

I looked down the hall and in the light of Hewitt's flashlight, I could just make out Helga. She was wearing a long white nightgown beneath her shearling coat, satin slippers on her feet. Her hair was loose for once and hung darkly around her pale face. I thought she looked a little like me, if I was thinner, but her nose was longer and her brow was higher and her head a bit larger than my own.

She was raking her hand through her hair and glancing over her shoulder as if afraid she was being watched.

Hewitt glanced over his shoulder too, then, in my direction, and saw me.

"She's all alone," he said, stepping backward. "She's scared of the dark and wants to know if she can stay the night."

"Where's Gia?" I asked, moving toward them.

Helga smiled at me slightly. She looked both prettier and

more ravaged without makeup. "I left her with the baby phone."
She held up half of a baby monitor. "She'll be fine. It's a very
powerful device. I'll hear her if she cries."

"But isn't it electric?" I said.

"No. Batteries," Helga said.

"I mean the part that sits near her crib. The base. Isn't that
electric?"

Helga looked at me. "So?"

"There's a blackout," I said. "It won't work without elec-
tricity."

Helga let out a heavy sigh. "Oh. I guess I'll just have to go
get her. Hewitt, can you lend me a hand?"

I waited in the doorway for them to return. After a few minutes, they did, Hewitt lugging a portable crib in one hand, pillows under the other arm. Helga carried the baby wrapped in a
blanket. Gia was rubbing her eyes and whimpering, still not
fully awake.

"Rachel, this is so kind of you," Helga said, sweeping past
me. "Don't worry," she said. "The couch will be fine. Gia can
sleep in the Pack 'n Play beside me."

Our apartment was small—we'd turned the smaller bedroom
into a combination nursery-office—leaving just the living room,
dining area, kitchen, and our bedroom. It was colorful and cozy
and not very chic. Now, lit by candles, it looked even cozier.

In the dim light, Helga placed Gia in the Pack 'n Play and
began to make the couch into a bed for herself with a crisp
efficiency.

While she busied herself, I whispered to Hewitt that I needed to speak to him alone in our bedroom.

"What is going on here?" I asked, when the door was closed. "What is she doing here?"

"I don't know," Hewitt whispered back. He held a single candle that lit his face from beneath, casting shadows in such a way that he looked like a phantom. "She has a serious phobia about the dark. She told me earlier when I was setting up the high chair." He shrugged. "What else can we do?"

"Um, lend her some candles and tell her to go home?"

Hewitt looked unhappy but nodded. I followed him into the living room. Helga was just lying down on the sofa, pulling the blanket she'd brought up to her chin. Gia, in the Pack 'n Play beside her, was standing, holding the rail of the crib and looking around, confused.

"Helga," Hewitt said. "Listen, the thing is—"

There was a loud beep then from the microwave and all the lights and machines in the house came on.

Gia began to cry, a long, slow wail like a siren.

"I guess they fixed the problem," Hewitt said.

Helga sighed heavily and started to get up but stopped and tilted her head forward.

It took me a moment to realize she was crying. After a moment, she lifted her head and her face was all streaked with tears and snot.

"I'm so alone," she said over the cries of Gia. "I want to go home. Why did I even come here?"

"You were afraid of the dark," Hewitt said.

"No, not here. I mean America. Why did I come to this country?" She had been looking between the two of us, but now she looked squarely at Hewitt. "Do you really think I'm beautiful? Honestly. Am I?"

Hewitt glanced at me and tried to smile as if this were all part of some private joke we'd shared, but I just stared back.

Helga didn't wait for an answer, but went on, still weeping. "Dave despises me," she said. "I really think he wishes I was dead. We haven't touched each other in months."

Beside her, Gia was wailing. "Tata, Tata," she cried, over and over again.

Helga glanced at the baby and said something fast and guttural in German. When the child didn't respond, Helga looked at me and said, "Will you shut her up, please?"

I went and picked her up. I held her close, making soft clucking noises. I heard George beginning to whimper. Still holding Gia, I made my way to the nursery.

By the time I got there, George had settled himself back to sleep. Gia's cries had subsided but she was still sniffling, and she let out little shuddering sounds as she burrowed her head into my neck.

Through the wall I could hear the muted voices of Helga and Hewitt. I knew I should go back to them. I knew I should go see what was going on in the brightness of that living room. But the nursery was dark and warm and they seemed somehow abstract out there, unreal, like an old movie playing on the television.

George was asleep again, snoring on his belly, his butt stuck in the air. I sat down in the rocker with Gia. The night-light was on, so I could see her face. She was, I realized in that half-light, a beautiful child. I hadn't seen it before. She had in fact inherited the best of both her parents. But her eyes were dark pools of sadness, and she was gripping the edge of my nightgown, her bottom lip pushed out as if she was about to start crying again.

I felt wetness against my skin, and when I looked down, I saw that I was leaking milk. It seeped outward, making my nightgown transparent, revealing my areola, brown and wide, through the thin fabric.

I pulled my gown open and Gia moved in and began to suckle. I felt my milk let down and I saw her eyes flutter upward with the first mouthful.

I could still hear their voices out there. I could hear Helga asking that question over and over again through her tears, a voice both desperate and detached, "Do you really think I'm beautiful? Do you really?"